KITH AND KIN

Recent Titles by Jane A. Adams from Severn House

The Naomi Blake Mysteries

MOURNING THE LITTLE DEAD
TOUCHING THE DARK
HEATWAVE
KILLING A STRANGER
LEGACY OF LIES
SECRETS
GREGORY'S GAME
PAYING THE FERRYMAN
A MURDEROUS MIND
FAKES AND LIES

The Rina Martin Mysteries

A REASON TO KILL
FRAGILE LIVES
THE POWER OF ONE
RESOLUTIONS
THE DEAD OF WINTER
CAUSE OF DEATH
FORGOTTEN VOICES

Henry Johnstone Mystery

THE MURDER BOOK
DEATH SCENE
KITH AND KIN

KITH AND KIN

Jane A. Adams

This first world edition published 2018
in Great Britain and 2019 in the USA by
SEVERN HOUSE PUBLISHERS LTD of
Eardley House, 4 Uxbridge Street, London W8 7SY
Trade paperback edition first published
in Great Britain and the USA 2019 by
SEVERN HOUSE PUBLISHERS LTD

British Library Cataloguing in Publication Data
A CIP catalogue record for this title is available from the British Library.

ISBN-13: 978-0-7278-8827-3 (cased)
ISBN-13: 978-1-84751-953-5 (trade paper)
ISBN-13: 978-1-4483-0162-1 (e-book)

All Severn House titles are printed on acid-free paper.

Severn House Publishers support the Forest Stewardship Council™ [FSC™],
the leading international forest certification organisation.
All our titles that are printed on FSC certified paper carry the FSC logo.

Typeset by Palimpsest Book Production Ltd.,
Falkirk, Stirlingshire, Scotland.
Printed and bound in Great Britain by
TJ International, Padstow, Cornwall.

PROLOGUE

December 1918

'I'm sorry,' he said, though he sounded anything but apologetic, 'but we had to kill your husband. We can't be doing with liars.'

The woman faced him across the scrubbed wooden table. She didn't speak but her hands, resting on the back of a chair, clutched at the rail so tightly that her knuckles blanched. Her husband's chair, he guessed, set at the head of the table and the best piece of furniture to be seen in this small but immaculately clean kitchen.

'No reason you should be blamed, of course. Boss knows you had nothing to do with it. Your old man was always a bit of a—'

He paused as she lifted a hand to silence him and seemed about to speak.

He waited, but she had obviously thought better of it and he continued as though there had been no pause. 'So long as you and the young 'uns clear out tonight, pack your things and leave without a fuss, no more'll be said and you can go and start again somewhere else. Boss has provided for you and there's a cart waiting outside to take you into town.'

'But this is our home.'

He glanced briefly at the young girl who stood beside her mother, eyes round and scared but indignant too. He'd spied her younger brother standing uncertainly in the kitchen doorway when he and his men had come in.

'You be quiet when your elders are talking,' he told the girl. She looked to her mother for support, but the woman, older and wiser, had more sense than to answer back.

'You'd best go and pack,' he said. 'I'll wait in here. Tommy will go with you, carry your bags.' *And make sure you behave*, he could have added.

For the briefest moment she looked up and met his gaze, her expression carefully blank, but he could feel the simmering hatred behind the cold control and for a fleet second he felt the threat of it.

He shifted his weight and gestured to Thomas to go with the woman. 'Best be getting on with it, then,' he said. 'Done is done and no sense in waiting for it to change.'

She did not move immediately, not liking to be bossed around in her own home, now that the only person she acknowledged had the right to do that was gone, but then she went off quietly enough, taking the boy and girl up the stairs with her. He stood in the kitchen, listening to the sounds of cupboards opening and the rough note of Tommy's boots on the wooden boards, heavier than either woman or child; all three of them went soft shod in the house. He'd noted their boots set in a row by the door of the back porch when he'd arrived. Noted too that there was space for a fourth pair: those of the man now gone.

They loaded the bags and baggage into the waiting cart and Tommy lifted the boy up to sit beside him on the bench. Mother and daughter sat on their bags in the body of the wagon. All three had blankets, draped like cloaks over their winter clothes.

Tommy set off, following his boss's car. A cold December wind blew in across the Medway, carrying the first flurries of snow. Until now the season had been wet and miserable, but the temperature was falling and promised a drier cold.

The woman sat like a statue, unmoving, staring out into the dark, but the girl gazed back the way they had come and the boy craned round in his seat on the driving bench as they watched their cottage burn.

ONE

December 1928

The two bodies lay about twenty feet apart on the mud flats. The receding tide had dropped them unceremoniously on the shoreline further up towards the mouth of Otterham Creek and, according to the sailorman who had spotted them and dragged them to this end of the creek, beyond the reaches and the tidal flow, it was likely that they'd been dumped in the Medway further upriver. The ebb and flow of several tides had probably brought them to rest on that bend, in the shallows at the edge of the water. The man gave his name as Frederick Garth. He and his boy, he said, had been unable to haul them safe to shore where they had first been spotted. They had used their tiny boat and, with the man handling the single oar and the boy keeping tight hold of the boat hook looped and twisted into clothing, brought them laboriously further into the creek. Eventually they had found a spot where they could bring the bodies ashore and had hauled them out with boat hooks; the mud showed clearly their passage through the stinking silt. But, the skipper told the silent and rather austere looking policeman, he'd tried not to disturb them more than he had to, grabbing the dead men by their belts and pulling hard in to shore. He'd touched nothing else and neither had the boy. He'd spotted them floating, he said, adding more detail in a vain attempt to elicit a response. He and the boy had dropped anchor, got themselves into the boat, and the boy had caught hold with the boat hook while he'd hauled in to shore. Then they'd gone back for the other. Two trips they'd made in as many hours, the bodies dragging in the water something fierce and the boy, not having the strength of a grown man, had struggled with the task.

'And no blame on him for that,' the man said fiercely, the lack of response rousing him to anger. 'He almost lost hold, so we drifted a little off course on the second run.' He spread his arms wide to indicate the distance between the two bodies on the foreshore. 'But he did his best, the lad did.'

Getting very little response from the man he understood to be a detective inspector, he turned to the shorter, broader and more forthcoming companion.

'It was hard to hold our course. You c'n see that for yoursen. So one ended up there and the other over yon.'

'You did a fine job,' Mickey reassured him. 'I wouldn't have known how or where to begin. Neither of us would, not having your skills.'

The sailorman clearly had no doubt of that. He nodded rapidly. 'Then we had to go to the farm for help. They sent to the constable and he had a telephone and brought you here, but if you've done with us, suh, we'll be going. I've got the load to deliver and the wind is shifting. I'll be losing pay.'

Mickey Hitchens, detective sergeant with His Majesty's Metropolitan Police, nodded agreement. 'You'd best be going.' The man had already been delayed for too long, waiting for Mickey and his boss to make their slow way from London to Rainham and then from Rainham to this godforsaken spot.

The man stomped off and the boy, about ten or twelve years old, Mickey judged, made to follow. Mickey beckoned him over. He slipped a few coins into the boy's hand. 'Give these to your master,' he said. 'Compensation for his lost time.'

The boy clenched his hand around the coins and ran off to join his elder. Mickey watched him go and then turned his attention back to the two bodies.

His boss, Chief Inspector Henry Johnstone, had bent from his great height and crouched over the closest of them. 'You should have told him to fill out a compensation form,' he said wryly.

'And have them wait six months just to have the claim rejected? They say no good deed goes unpunished. He could have left well alone and we'd have been none the wiser. As it is, he's lost time, and time means pay.'

Henry considered and then nodded slowly. He stood, drawing his heavy coat, a recent gift from his sister, tightly across his chest. The hem had dragged in the mud and Henry flicked at it ineffectually with a gloved hand. A damp and bitter wind blew in across the water, loaded with moisture from way out at sea, and the gathering clouds, Mickey thought, presaged an equally cold and bitter rain.

'We should get them moved,' Mickey said. 'Soon as we can before the weather turns. If they've washed down from upstream, there's not much we can learn from here.'

'If,' Henry said, but he nodded. The boatman knew the river; chances were he was right. Henry too looked up at the sky, black clouds roiling and twisting into thunderheads. 'We'll get them packed up and into the wagon and we'll head back. You recognize him?' He gestured towards the body he had been examining.

'I do indeed,' Mickey said. 'Billy Crane, one of Bailey's men. I'm guessing the other will have a similar provenance.'

He extended a hand to his boss and hauled him back on to the firmer ground of the bank. They had brought wellington boots with them and Henry's were caked in foul smelling mud, almost to the tops.

Mickey beckoned to the local constable and gave instructions for the removal of the dead men. The man looked worried.

'You need extra hands,' Mickey told him. 'We'll gladly lend them.'

The constable looked even more troubled at the thought of his superiors helping out. 'Thank you, sir, but my lads can manage that. Trouble is, if we load both bodies into the cart, I'm not so sure the horse can handle them as well as your two good selves, not over such sucking ground. I can send one of the lads to rustle up some extra transport?'

Mickey shook his head. 'It's only a mile or so back to the road, Constable. The inspector and I, we're well used to walking. You see to the dead; the living will make shift for themselves.'

The constable looked from Mickey to the senior detective and then back again. A more direct glance from Mickey prompted Henry, reminding him that he ought to make a response.

'Walking back will do us no harm, Constable. But you and your men had best make shift before the weather closes in.'

The constable, finally reassured, nodded and made off back to where the bodies lay, his three associates in tow.

'Best move ourselves, sharpish,' Mickey observed. 'We're in for a soaking, that's for sure.'

Henry nodded and turned away from the scene of activity by the river, settling his hat more firmly on his head. Over their serge uniforms the uniformed officers wore heavy oilskin capes which would hamper their movements in bringing the bodies to the cart but stand them in good stead for the walk, escorting the wagon back to the settlement of Upchurch where it had been arranged to lodge the bodies in the church overnight until proper transport could be arranged to take them to the railway. The farmer whose cart they'd borrowed would have a longer journey and the sacking he had used to swathe his head and shoulders would be soaked through by the time he reached home. They'd best give him something for his trouble as well, Henry thought.

A car, the one and only allocated to the Kent Constabulary, had been sent to fetch them from the station and had brought them to a point a mile outside Upchurch, but it had been obvious it would be of little use thereafter and they had left it and the driver back on what passed for a main road. Mickey, feeling the first drops of heavy rain sliding down the back of his neck, was relieved to think they'd not have to walk the entire way back. He fell into step beside his boss. His friend.

'So what are two of Josiah Bailey's men doing right out here, in the back of beyond?'

'Not so far from his usual ground, I suppose,' Henry argued. 'This might feel like the back of beyond but we're only a scant few miles from Rochester and Sittingbourne and Rainham, and those towns are only a train ride from the East End. Josiah Bailey has contacts and probably family hereabouts. Besides, we still don't know where they went into the water. The Medway is a powerful river.'

'And one I don't know so well. If they'd fetched up in the Thames, I could make a guess as to where they might have been pitched into the water. Bailey's not going to be too happy about it.'

'Unless he ordered it. He's known to have a short fuse, even with his own people. Even with his own kin, for that matter.'

Mickey nodded. Josiah Bailey had ordered his own cousin killed not six months before, or so the rumour mill had it. And over a woman . . . though Mickey was inclined to take that part with a pinch of salt. New women were two a penny to a man like Bailey and anyone else who fancied their chances, so it was said, just had to wait in patience until Bailey grew tired of his latest. Bailey and his family had been ruling over their little bit of the East End since before the war. Gambling, women, protection money all added to the family wealth and, Mickey supposed, a kind of prestige. They certainly ruled their little kingdom with tight fists. Mickey and Inspector Johnstone had engaged in several run-ins with the Bailey family; the latest, only the previous autumn, had resulted in their taking Josiah Bailey briefly into custody. Now he was in the wind and neither Henry nor Mickey had heard news of him in several months.

The rain had started to fall and Mickey glanced back towards the river. From the look of it, they had one body in the cart and were bringing up the other. He turned up his collar and settled his hat more squarely on his head as the cold and heavy drops began to fall in earnest.

'Crane had a blow to the head, though that could easily have been *post mortem*, and a stab wound to the chest. I thought I discerned a bullet wound in the chest of the second body but there is so much mud it's difficult to tell. We will have to see if your photographs can tell us more.'

Mickey nodded. He glanced back once more towards the river. The rain was falling so viciously now that he could only just make out the cart and the constables moving up the path, heads down and shoulders hunched. Flat land, Mickey thought. Flat and bleak and sodden and, no doubt, dangerous too. They'd been warned to keep to the path. It was getting toward dusk and in the heavy rain it was easy to miss your footing and stumble into one of the many creeks and inlets that criss-crossed this landscape. It was definitely not to Mickey's taste.

At last, through the gloom, Mickey sighted the shape of a car. Spotting them, the driver leapt out and hurried to assist them. They stripped off wellington boots and dumped them in the duffel Mickey had used to carry them from London. This and the murder bag and his camera were laid hastily in the rear footwell and the two men scrambled to get out of the storm.

'So,' Henry picked up their earlier conversation as the driver sought to keep the car on the narrow and increasingly treacherous track. 'Two of Bailey's men, or so we assume. Both dumped in the river, so possibly some effort at concealment. Bailey has a tendency to display his dead, let them serve as a warning to others not to cross him. That, in my mind, lessens the likelihood of them being dead by his orders.'

'You're thinking about Albert Lines.'

Mickey nodded. Lines had been a pawnbroker, one of many who acted as fences and middlemen. He had tried to fiddle his payments to Bailey and Bailey had him killed. Sent his men to cut the hands off Albert Lines and leave him to bleed out in the street, threatening similar treatment to anyone who made to help the unfortunate man.

'Among others. Lines was unlucky. There are signs that Bailey's hold hasn't been as tight recently as it once was. Ted Grieves tried a similar trick and seems to have survived the exercise.'

Ted Grieves had been suspected of skimming a little too much profit. 'Ted Grieves has also dropped off the face of the earth. He could be dead as well, for all we know.'

'But not made an example of. Even before Bailey himself went on the run, there were indications that there was less iron in his fist.'

'And not a hide nor hair seen of him since October,' Mickey added ruefully. It grieved him severely that they'd had Bailey in their hands and then lost him. The last sighting of their man had been an unconfirmed report of him getting on a train at Paddington station. There had been no word of him getting off said train, and Mickey was now inclined to view the report as at best a mistake and at worst a case of mischief-making.

'We'll get a better handle on things once we know who the other fellow is,' he said.

* * *

They had reached Upchurch and the driver pulled in at the door of the Crown Inn.

'I drove back here while you were seeing to the bodies, sir,' he said, addressing Henry Johnstone. 'Sorted out accommodation for the both of you. The landlord, Mr James Falkner, he's getting two rooms ready for you, said he'd get the fires going and a meal for this evening.'

'Thank you for that,' Henry said. 'Constable Hargreaves and the rest of the men, do they have further to go?'

'Constable's local, sir. Lives in Upchurch. I've sorted out a van and driver to take the rest back. I hope that was appropriate, sir.'

'Very appropriate,' Henry told him. 'And the bodies will be taken to the church?'

'Room is being made in the sacristy,' the driver assured him.

Content that nothing more could be done, Henry helped Mickey with their bags and they hurried inside. He felt chilled now, his back aching and his hands numb, despite the gloves and the warm coat Cynthia had been generous enough to buy for him. He did not deal so well with cold and damp these days. Too much of it in the trenches seemed to have lowered his resistance and as he got older, so the damp seemed to settle further into his bones.

Older, Henry thought wryly. At forty-two he was hardly decrepit as yet, but there were days when he felt as ancient as Methuselah. Smaller and squarer than Henry, Mickey seemed as inured to the chill as the brick wall he resembled.

James Falkner came to greet them as they came into the bar. The Crown was not yet open for evening trade but Falkner had a fire going and offered tea and hot toddies, both of which Mickey accepted on their behalf.

'And I can rustle up some bread and cheese, maybe a bit of home-made pickle? It's a while till supper will be ready.'

Mickey thanked him. 'That would be very welcome,' he said. He steered Henry towards the fire and dumped their bags, removing his coat and dropping it over the back of a chair to dry. 'Off with your coat,' he told Henry, who had slumped down into one of the two wing chairs set beside the blaze and looked disinclined to move.

Henry, miles away, looked up in surprise.

'Your coat,' Mickey said. 'It needs to dry out, and so do you.'

Henry sighed and shrugged out of his overcoat. Mickey hung that beside his own, the steam already rising and a smell of wet dog permeating the air.

'How much sleep have you had this past week?'

'Enough,' Henry replied sharply. Then he relented. 'Not much,' he admitted.

Mickey nodded. 'Anniversaries are hard,' he said.

'And there are too many damned anniversaries.'

'Isn't that the truth.'

The landlord and a girl bustled in and set food and drink on tables beside their guests and then left them alone. 'Eat,' Mickey ordered. 'I'm bloody starved. You must be too.'

TWO

1918

Rainham was silent as the strange little procession – an old, beaten-up cart following a brown Siddeley-Deasy coupé – rattled into town and turned into Station Road.

Tommy halted the cart in front of the station entrance. It was a spare, scant place, and looked deserted at this time of the evening. He helped the passengers down from the cart, just as a distant church clock struck nine. It was raining; cold, heavy drops mixed with halfhearted snow, and it was bitterly cold. The children shivered and Dalla hugged them close.

'I'll be leaving you here,' Tommy said. 'I expect there'll be someone in the ticket office who can help you . . . Best I don't know where you're going.' He placed a bag at Dalla's feet. 'There's money in there. Enough to take you . . . wherever . . . and see you right until you can get back on your feet.'

'Blood money,' Dalla said flatly.

'Call it what you want, it'll still spend just as well.'

Dalla made no reply.

Tommy climbed back on to the cart and watched as Dalla and the children entered the station. She'd picked up the bag, he noted, but she was known to be a sensible woman and would be conscious of her duty to the living. There was no more to be done for the dead.

He felt a certain sympathy for her and a certain interest too. Dalla Beaney was a good-looking woman, despite the two kids and the man who had been a bit too handy with his fists at times. Tommy didn't hold with hitting women. Kids neither, if it came to that. He wondered if she'd miss her old man or if she'd be grateful that he'd gone. She'd thrived just fine while he'd been away at the war. Word was that he'd come back angrier and meaner than ever, though.

Tommy clucked his tongue at the horses and urged them

on. He wrapped the oilskin more tightly around his shoulders and tugged his scarf more snugly beneath his cap and then turned the cart back in the direction he'd come, hoping to have the cart returned and be off home again before midnight.

He watched, enviously, as Billy Crane took off in the car, heading the other way to make his report to Josiah senior. Young Jo had wanted to come along tonight and Tommy had been a little surprised at the vehemence with which his father had ordered him to remain behind.

Tommy glanced back over his shoulder, still thinking about the woman. If she'd the sense he credited her with, she'd be miles away by morning, put this all behind her and start over, maybe find herself another man. It wouldn't be hard, Tommy thought, to find a better man than her Manfrid had been. He wished her luck with it.

Dalla waited until she was certain that the men had gone.

'Ma?'

'Hush, child. It will all be well.'

'But, Ma—'

'I said to hush,' Dalla told her daughter firmly. 'Come now.'

'Are we not waiting for the train?' Kem asked.

'No,' Dalla told him. 'We'll not be catching the train.' She straightened up, looking compassionately at both her children. They were cold and tired, and no doubt grieving. Grieving was what you did when someone told you that your father was dead and gone, even if the four years he'd been absent were so much better than those they could recall when he'd been there. She had pulled blankets off their beds and wrapped them around skinny shoulders before the children had been lifted into the cart. Brought a warm shawl for herself and tucked it around her, beneath her coat. They look like waifs and strays, she thought, as she tugged the blankets more tightly around the young boy and girl. Kem, trying to be the tough boy, wriggled away and she clucked her tongue at him in reprimand. He stilled beneath her hands and allowed her to tuck him in.

'There'll be no one to see on the road we're taking. So best be warm,' she told him, securing the blanket with a large pin.

'Where are we going, Ma? If we ain't getting on the train, then?'

Dalla shook her head at her daughter's question. 'We walk,' she said. 'Family.' She nodded firmly. 'When you're in need, you go to family, you don't take off on the first train that comes along. You don't just run.'

'Family?' Malina asked her. She sounded anxious.

'My family. Not his,' Dalla told her. 'We go back to where I came from. They'll take us in. That's what family do.'

She hefted the two larger bags and left the children to divide up the smaller packs between themselves. Sometimes, she reflected, it was best that you didn't own much. At least there was less to carry. She led them out of the station and studied the road. It would be a long walk and the night was filthy. Best be starting, then.

Dalla set off, striding out with more confidence than she actually felt, knowing that her children needed her strength. 'We've a good way to go,' she said, not quite certain just how far. 'Be brave now, I know you can both do this, my loves.'

Brother and sister looked at one another, reluctant to leave the shelter of the station for the blasting wind and chilling rain. Kem reached out for Malina's hand, suddenly more child than man. His sister, two years older, took her lead from their mother and clasped his fingers, lending what strength she had left. The streets were empty, anyone who had a home now tucked up inside with doors locked and curtains drawn.

No one saw them leave.

THREE

1928

It had taken Henry a very long time to warm up. He'd still been shivering when he and Mickey went up to their rooms and Mickey's advice had been to partake of a second hot toddy and then get some rest before supper. The bodies had been laid out on trestle tables in the sacristy – the constable had popped into the inn for long enough to tell them that – and they had arranged to inspect them later in the evening, but there was little of use they could do until the morning. It was then only a little after four in the afternoon but the darkness was absolute. Dusk and rain blocking the light like a sodden blanket. The sacristy was lit only by paraffin lamps, the constable told them, not really adequate for carrying out a detailed inspection.

On the plus side, he had managed to obtain a van and driver to take the bodies to the station the next morning.

'So long as it can be done early,' the constable added. 'Jack has his rounds to do after, deliveries to make.'

Henry had been chilled and weary enough to take Mickey's advice. He had even slept for a time, waking after an hour, still tired but at least no longer chilled. He was fully aware that he would probably not get back to sleep again that night, especially not in a strange room and a strange bed.

The small room at the Crown was comfortable enough. A single bed with a thick counterpane and a chest of drawers, a washstand with a tiled splashback no longer used for its original purpose but now doubling as dressing table or desk. The bathroom and toilet were down the hall, as was Mickey's room. The faint scent of developing chemicals drifted under Henry's door and he guessed that Mickey had probably commandeered the bathroom to use as a darkroom. He hoped Mickey would remember to move the crime scene prints elsewhere to dry. In

Henry's experience, people were oddly averse to seeing images of murdered bodies in their bathrooms and sculleries; his sergeant frequently had to make use of any conveniently available space when they were away from home.

Home, Henry thought, realizing that for him central office in Scotland Yard was as much home as his little flat.

Henry's small flat looked out over the Thames and he rarely closed the living room curtains, preferring to be able to see the lights and activity of a thoroughfare that was never really silent and certainly never still. At night, it was mainly steam vessels that made their way upriver; the sailing barges that still came this far upstream would wait until daylight, moored up until the tide turned or until the tugs could bring them safely under the bridges, mainsails down and masts lowered. He thought about the man and boy who had found the bodies and wondered idly if they had reached their destination and unloaded their cargo. Once they'd offloaded, they were bound for the Blue Circle cement works in the Medway, Mickey had told him, shipping their cargo to the West Country and most likely bringing china clay back. It must be a strange life, Henry thought, these small ships, crewed by a man and boy or a captain and two hands, one usually still technically a child fresh out of school. They plied their trade up and down the coast, sometimes even venturing across the shipping lanes to the coasts of northern France.

Childhood, Henry thought, ended all too swiftly for most children, especially the children of the poor. Henry and his sister, though his family had endured no such acute financial pressures, had also had their own childhood curtailed, in their case by a father who saw no value in creatures who could not contribute to his own wellbeing. Then the father had died and it had just been Henry and Cynthia and, all things considered, they had done well; in their case it was better to be parentless than so badly parented.

Henry's jacket hung on the bedpost and he fumbled in the pocket for his notebook and then leaned back against the pillows. At home he would have settled comfortably in his favourite chair, set beside the window. The chair was old and the leather worn soft. He fed it regularly, polishing it with a soft cloth and leather food to keep the cracked surface supple. He missed his chair and missed the soft, tartan rug he left on the arm.

Making do, he tugged the counterpane across his legs and began to write.

Josiah Bailey. What did he know about Josiah Bailey?

> *Born in Fournier Street, if I remember correctly, and lived, until September of this year, only a few streets away from the house in which he was born. That house is now occupied by a cousin and most of the street is occupied by Bailey's family or by those who serve his family in one capacity or another.*
>
> *Bailey was born into a life of criminality. The second of three brothers, with two sisters.*

Was that right? Henry wondered. He could recall the names of two sisters, but had a vague thought that there might have been a third.

His older brother was lost at Ypres. The second returned but died of his injuries. Bailey served. Henry made a note to examine his army records more closely, surprised at the random details he recalled about the rest of Bailey's family.

So this left Josiah Bailey as the sole heir to the rackets that his father, Josiah Bailey senior, had already established, the sisters having been married to trusted associates.

Henry paused, trying to recall what he had been told about these marriages. One sister, he thought – Pauline, if he remembered correctly – had been married at seventeen or eighteen to one of her father's lieutenants, and the other, he thought, had actually moved away. The mother had died shortly after the war had ended. Died of grief, it was said. Henry was quite prepared to accept that; he'd seen too many men and women fade and depart, the light having gone from their lives far too soon.

Henry paused with the pen raised above the page, thinking suddenly about his own sister. What would Cynthia do if another war were to come and her sons were conscripted? Henry knew that his sister would fight tooth and nail to keep her children safe. She had fought like a demon to protect herself and Henry, so he was fully aware of her capacities.

Unable to cope with the impact of it, Henry thrust the thought aside. There would not be another conflict. The one in which he had fought was meant to be the war to end all wars, wasn't it?

He dragged his thoughts back to Josiah Bailey.

Since about 1920, Josiah Bailey senior has gradually handed over the reins of power to his son. In the past five years this devolvement has become more rapid due to the ill health of the older man. It is reported that he has now rescinded all control and is in effective retirement, though rumour has it he can still make his wrath felt when someone displeases him. Other rumours surmise that he is already dead, and some accuse the son of helping him on his way.

It is not unusual to hear that one of the Bailey gang is suddenly unaccounted for. In the main, bodies are rarely found, unless Bailey junior wishes to make a point.

Henry turned his thoughts to the man he had identified. Billy Crane was a long-term associate and known to be a favoured employee of the younger Bailey.

Billy Crane. Housebreaker, rumoured to be a cracksman, though I can't recall he has ever been brought in on suspicion of that particular service. Not a big or particularly violent man. Not one of Bailey's heavies. As I recall, he is in his late twenties. Bailey himself is forty-three and his father must now be well into his seventies.

Bailey is not a big man; not physically. Of medium height and solid but not heftily built. He is known to be strong for his size and not averse to using that strength. When he wishes to make an example, Josiah Bailey is not a man afraid to dirty his own hands.

He must have served in the war, but I do not recall reading about his army record.

Henry paused, his thoughts returning to the victims. Billy Crane was not a stupid man. Henry had encountered him on several occasions. He said little, implicated no one; unlike many of his associates he was not known to run off at the mouth under pressure.

Grew up on the same street as the Baileys, as I recall. Related in some way?

A knock at the door interrupted his thoughts and Mickey came in carrying two wooden trays, one stacked atop the other, the photographs laid out on each one buffered by the handles. He set them down on the bed and then plonked down beside them.

'You warmed up yet?'

'I am. Yes.'

'Good. I thought I'd make myself busy and get these out of the way and processed. Not, I think, that they'll be a lot of use to us, except to remind us just how bleak and drear this place is and that we shouldn't come here looking for pleasure.'

Henry turned one of the trays towards him and studied the images. Mickey handed him a glass. The landscape had been a monochrome of browns and greys but the photographs, small black and white contact prints, reduced what little there had been in terms of other tones and just served to reinforce the sense of bleakness and emptiness.

Mud and reeds and water. Heavy sky, all stark shades of black and grey, and the two bodies resting on the cold, sucking mud. The bodies themselves looked broken, weighed down by earth and water as though, had they waited only a little longer, they might have disappeared into the marsh and be gone for ever, with none the wiser.

Henry took the glass and studied the faces. Billy Crane he knew, even though the face had begun to bloat and the eyes were fishlike and dead. Henry had examined the hands at the scene and the skin on the fingers was already loosening. He reckoned they might have been in the water two or three days but no more. He turned his attention to the other man and felt a vague sense of recognition but could not place him. It would be difficult to take fingerprints from either body, he guessed, and so they'd be relying on mug shots for identification.

Possibly dental records, but Henry knew from experience that many in the working classes did not or could not afford to attend a dentist.

He cast an eye over the rest of the pictures and then asked, 'Did you take any wide shots? Looking out towards the sea?'

Mickey looked slightly surprised, but nodded. 'I did, but I've not printed them yet. You can take a look at the negatives.' He went to fetch them, pointing out the ones that might be of most interest, and Henry held them up to the gas light. He was silent for several moments and then he said, 'Where's the boat?'

'The rowing boat? That's—'

'No, the sailing barge. They said they dropped anchor at the mouth of the creek when they spotted the bodies. We should be able to see it. The weather didn't close in until shortly before we left.'

Mickey frowned. He took the negatives from his boss and studied them carefully. 'I could have missed it.'

'You've taken a panorama of shots,' Henry pointed out, 'as you always do.'

Since Henry owned the cameras that Mickey used and paid for the film, Mickey never skimped with his contextual shots, as many of the official photographers did. Henry believed that you should be able to view a crime scene from 360 degrees if at all possible and Mickey was of the same mind.

'There are no other shots, they're all here, either negatives or prints. Obviously I've only got contact prints, but no, you're right. Put these together and you'd have a complete panorama. I've not missed anything.' He sounded somewhat relieved though Henry had never been in any doubt.

'You don't miss things, Mickey,' he said. 'There is no boat.'

'It's a mass of little inlets around there; it could be we just can't see it. We need local eyes on this. Reliable ones,' he added. 'So, what are you thinking, that they lied from start to finish, or that they just lied about part of it?'

Henry got up and walked to the window. He drew the curtain aside and peered out. It was dark and the rain was still hammering down. 'I think there's very little we can do either way tonight. We get hold of the constable and talk to him.

He's coming at dawn to help supervise the shipment of the bodies.'

The plan had been that they would escort the two dead men back to London, but Mickey guessed that had changed. 'I'll tell the landlord that we're going to be staying on here another night.' He glanced at his pocket watch, stroking the smooth brass case as he always did. It was an old friend. 'Speaking of which, the landlord said supper would be ready for six and it's almost that now.'

Henry nodded and picked up his jacket from the end of the bed. 'So, why go to all that trouble for a lie? If someone wanted to dispose of the bodies, all they had to do was let the sea take them. Besides, you and I have both seen them – they'd not been placed in the water in the last few hours; the skin has started to slough off the hands and is slack on the faces. Something had already had a go at the eyes, and abrasions and tears to the clothing suggest the river had held on to them for a time.'

'The man was quick enough to give us his schedule. Cement factory, then around the coast to Cornwall, back with a load of china clay. In my experience, if people want to lie, they fall back on what might be half truths. Most folk are not good at making up a full story.'

'True,' Henry agreed. 'So we assume there is some truth in the story,' he added, as they both made for the stairs. 'I expect you photographed them both.'

'Did it without thinking,' Mickey agreed. 'I doubt either of the pair noticed.'

'Good. I think we have more of a mystery here than just the finding of two dead men.'

'Well, when we've eaten we'll make our way across to the church and see what we can see, now they've dried out a bit.'

The church clock was striking seven when they made their way between whitewashed cottages in narrow streets to the Church of St Mary, bringing the keys which had been dropped off at the Crown for them.

The church sat low and long, snuggled into the landscape. It was too dark to see but the landlord had told them that it had an unusual stepped steeple, the top section swivelled and settled like a candle snuffer on top of a steeple candle.

Apparently, in land so low lying as this, even this long low church could be seen from the sea and the strange steeple, with its octagonal top, acted as a landmark.

'Sir Francis Drake's father was vicar here,' Mickey commented as he opened the door.

'No wonder he was in such a hurry to leave,' Henry said.

'Unkind. It's a nice enough place. You just have a fit of the grouches because it's made you cold.'

Henry's coat was nearly dry. The landlord had left both his and Mickey's by the fire until the pub opened for the evening trade, and he was grateful of it now. Outside it was bleak and the sacristy was no warmer when they let themselves in. The local vicar, they'd been told, was away with a dying parishioner, but the sacristan was available, should they need him. Mr Falkner, the landlord, had told them that the sacristan was not happy about bodies being dumped in his church without his leave. Henry judged that Falkner was amused by this.

'So,' he said, 'Billy Crane.' He watched as Mickey began a more thorough examination than the one they'd been able to make on the foreshore. Mickey was careful not to disturb the body more than they had to – the most thorough examination would be made at the post-mortem – but he drew the jacket aside and examined the chest of the late Billy Crane. 'Stab wound?' This was what Henry had noticed earlier.

'Looks like it. Quite a broad blade, I'm guessing. But of course that's hard to tell; the lips of the wound draw back in the hours and days after death. No sign of rigor mortis; could have come and gone, or could have been delayed because of the cold water. I'll place that question in the hands of those more expert. But looking at the hands,' – he held one of Billy Crane's hands for Henry's inspection – 'I'd say our guess is about right. Two, possibly three days, but certainly no more. The skin is lifted and is beginning to slough, but it feels as though it is still connected to the inner layers of flesh. Of course, the chill of the water is an unpredictable factor.'

He paused, noticing something, and pushed back the cuff

of the jacket. 'Look. He's been bound. Tight. And there are clear rope marks.'

Henry took the hand and inspected the wrist more closely. 'I think most of this bruising is *post mortem*,' he said. 'For the blood to have settled like this, taking on the pattern of the rope weave, I think it's likely that he was left bound for a time, after he had been killed.'

Mickey examined the second man, finding similar marks on his wrists.

'I thought I saw a bullet wound, but it was hard to tell with all the mud.'

Mickey turned his attention to the man's chest. 'Well, for my money it's another stab wound, but not from a knife. Or at least not from anything with a flat blade.'

Henry came over and studied the wound, understanding now why he had mistaken it. The wound was large and the edges rounded and drawn back. Now Mickey had wiped some of the mud away he could see that the sergeant was probably right. With Mickey's help, he lifted the body so that he could see the back. There was no sign of an exit wound, just what seemed to be a deep, rounded puncture.

'So, two stab wounds, in very similar places in the chest, but with different weapons. Two assailants, perhaps. And it's possible that both men were bound when the death blows were administered. This was not some bar fight or gang brawl. No one panicked and threw them in for the river to dispose of them. This was cold, Mickey.'

They checked pockets of jackets and trousers, but found nothing. An hour after they had arrived they left the sacristy and headed back to the Crown. Neither had much to say. They paused at the bar for a nightcap, aware of the stares and local interest. The pub was busy, quiet conversations, the sound of laughter. An easy place, relaxed and peaceful, but Henry could sense the undercurrent of unease. Even though the deaths had, in all likelihood, nothing to do with this community, when violent death chose to visit it sent ripples that took a long time to still.

Mickey was chatting to the barman; Mickey chatted to everyone with a nonchalance that Henry often envied. They seemed to be talking about employment and the importance of the brickworks. Henry sipped his drink and tuned it out, his thoughts wandering; he knew that if anything of note arose during the conversation Mickey would report back. It was nine o'clock when they went up to their rooms and Henry was dog tired. The brief doze in late afternoon had been helpful, but what he really needed was a sound night's sleep, and he doubted that that would be forthcoming.

They reached Henry's door first. 'Good night, then,' Mickey said. 'I told the landlord we'd be going across to the church first thing and then coming back for breakfast.'

Henry nodded and opened his door, then paused on the threshold. 'Mickey.'

His tone caused the sergeant to stop dead and come and look over his boss's shoulder. 'Bloody hell.'

Henry opened the door wider and took a step back out of the room so that Mickey could see more clearly. They had left the photographs on Henry's bed and Henry had locked the door, but now the bedroom window stood open, the room had been ransacked and the photographs were gone.

The landlord was mortified. Hargreaves, the constable they had met earlier, was summoned and now stood in the doorway, surveying the room.

'Well, it's a fine to-do and no mistake. What was taken, sir?'

He was an elderly man, and he had told them earlier that he should have been past retirement but was kept on because there was rarely any major demand on his services. He had spent his professional life dealing with the odd drunk and a few family disputes and young lads brawling in the street, but nothing like this.

'As far as I can tell,' Henry informed him, 'only the photographs that my colleague took at the crime scene today.'

The constable swung round, a look of shock on his face. 'That's what they came for? But how could they know . . .'

'My guess is that they came for the camera; it was pure luck for them that Sergeant Hitchens had set up a temporary darkroom and already done some of the printing.'

'And did they get the camera too?'

'Fortunately not. That was in Sergeant Hitchens' room and it seems whoever broke in did not manage to get *out* of mine. The door was locked from the outside, I'd taken the key with me, and though it looks as if they tried to break out, both door and lock are sturdy and they did not succeed.'

Henry indicated what looked like marks from a sharp blade wedged between the door and frame. Clearly someone had tried to lever the door open.

Henry crossed to the window. Mickey had dusted it for fingerprints and photographed the child-sized footprint on the sill and then Henry had had it pulled closed, but he opened it again now. 'As you see, it is a small window. There is a convenient downpipe that someone could have climbed up to reach it, but the window itself would not have allowed access for a man.'

'A boy, then. You think the man and the boy we saw today. The sailorman and his boy?'

'Can you think of a better explanation? My colleague took their photographs too. They must have realized that and not wanted to be recognized. Perhaps, although they appeared helpful, they were actually misleading us. Did you know them, Constable?'

Constable Hargreaves looked even more uncomfortable as he shook his head. 'Never seen either of them before. The boy went to Cooper's farm, that's where we borrowed the cart. Cooper called for me and I called for assistance, as seemed sensible. I sent word with the Coopers that we would need man and boy later but that you'd be some time in coming. I made a guess as to the time it would take Cooper to take the cart down. We all arrived, maybe an hour after that, it would have been just after noon, wouldn't it, sir? Cooper said the man and boy were already waiting for us when he got there.'

Henry consulted his notebook. 'And, according to the call that we received at central office, the bodies were discovered just after eight this morning?'

The constable was shaking his head vehemently. 'No, sir, they got that wrong. The bodies were finally *brought ashore* just after eight. Boatman said it took them a good couple of hours to tow them in.'

Henry closed his book and looked hard at the constable. 'So when they saw the bodies it would still have been dark. Saw them, identified what they were, made the decision to tow them in, launched their boat and spent two hours or so on the task. Take that back in time, Constable, and we are looking at an observation made from the sailing barge at around five thirty or six in the morning. At around six in the morning, at this time of the year, there is very little light to see anything by, never mind two sodden, dark-clad, most likely half submerged bodies in dark water. Nothing about the story struck you as odd? You gave no thought to where they might go to wait all this time, while you were contacting our central office in London and asking for the assistance of a detective?'

'I assumed they would go back to their barge,' the constable said a little testily. 'Forgive me, sir, but my time was taken up in contacting you, and then rustling up some other men who could come and assist at the scene. All of that took time. The first I saw was the first you saw. Man and boy and the two bodies lying on the mud of the foreshore. As you know, sir, the weather was closing in and the concern was just to get them out of there.'

Henry nodded, relenting a little. 'The constables you summoned, did any of them recognize the man and boy?'

'There were none that said so, but the only sailormen we see along here, in the Otterham Creek, are those that pull into the old wharves to take bricks on board or offload cement or lie up at Otterham Wharf. They come, they go, they rarely come ashore at that point. There's not so much for them out this way, not when they've only got a short way to go upriver to moor at Rochester or Chatham.'

'And did you see their boat? No doubt it would have been moored a little way out, perhaps at the entrance to the creek?'

From his expression, it was clear that the constable hadn't even looked, but then, Henry thought, neither had he. Assumptions had been made, natural but wrong assumptions, and as the constable said, with the weather rapidly closing in, they had all been keen to get out of the rain as quickly as possible.

'We had already planned to remain here for another day,'

Henry told him, 'and now it looks as though our stay might be extended further than that. In the morning when we have seen the bodies taken away, Constable, we will all return to Otterham Creek and get a better sense of the lie of the land and we'll speak to the Coopers. It could be that they can shed some light here.'

Henry dismissed the constable soon after and went to join Mickey, who had taken up residence again in the bathroom. He knocked on the door and was told to wait. Henry leaned against the wall and talked to his sergeant through the door. 'We've been made fools of,' he said.

'Perhaps. They didn't get the negatives, though, did they? I'd left the photographs on your bed, but all the negatives were back in my room and our housebreaker didn't get that far. They take anything else? Now that you've had a chance to check?'

'I had little with me,' Henry said, 'and there was nothing of value in the room. I wore my watch, my pen was in my coat, my lighter and tobacco tin too. They had emptied my clothes out on to the floor and cut the lining of my bag, but that can be mended with tape. It seemed my clothes were not worth their interest. My guess is, the boy was sent for the camera. My room is the only one that could have been reached so easily. No doubt he expected the door to be unlocked, so he was both lucky and unlucky. The window was simple enough to open. Any thin blade slid between frame and latch and the latch could be lifted from the exterior. There is no great security to this building.'

'You can come in now,' Mickey told him. The bathroom stank of developer and fix, both now somewhat stale and worked out so that the vinegar smell was even more acute. 'I've done what I can, but I need to be resupplied with the chemicals to do more. The prints are not as clean as I'd like, but they will do for now.'

He'd now made full sets of contact prints and they hung over the bath, dripping on to the enamel surface.

'And you still have pictures of man and boy.'

'I do indeed.' Mickey pointed them out and Henry peered closely.

'We've been taking too much at face value,' Henry said. 'I think both you and I were focused on the fact that these were Bailey's men, that we recognized one of them, that it is not unusual for men like that to turn up dead. That was all we saw.'

'That and the rain clouds,' Mickey added. 'There were none of us wanted to get a soaking, let's face it.'

Henry nodded. 'So now we look more closely and more carefully,' he said. 'We get the bodies shipped back to London in the morning, spend another day here and then return for the post-mortems. It could well be that we shall come back again but I'd like to set things in motion as far as photographs and fingerprints and any other evidence we can gather are concerned. The landlord is already so put out that I'm sure he'll not mind keeping our rooms for us, just in case.'

Mickey grinned at him. 'And now they've made fools of us . . .' he said.

'Oh, you can be sure I'd bear a grudge for that,' Henry said.

FOUR

The rain had let up a little by the following morning. Mickey and Henry were up just after five, and in the dark supervised the transfer of the bodies into the local delivery van. One of the constables rode up front with the driver and another kept the bodies company in the back. The arrangement was that they would be met at Gillingham station, at which point the driver would be freed for his normal rounds.

They went back to the Crown for an early breakfast and Constable Hargreaves joined them. The mood was subdued, Henry still smarting from the break-in and also from the sense that they had missed the obvious the day before. Mickey, as usual, was more pragmatic about events. There was in the sergeant's view no sense in regretting; you learned and you moved on, and the only thing that was bothering him that morning was that he was now short of film and completely out of chemicals for processing.

Breakfast with home-made sausages, fried potatoes left over from the previous evening and fresh eggs. Mickey and Constable Hargreaves did it full justice and even Henry ate well – for Henry. The single police car owned by the Kent Constabulary was not available that morning but the constable had managed to procure the loan of the vicar's Austin Seven, the vicar now being back from his death-watch and not likely to be needing it that day. The car would be able to take them some way, but there would still be a good walk ahead for everyone, through mud and across rough ground.

By eight thirty they were back at the place where they had first seen the bodies the previous day. A stiff breeze was keeping the rain at bay, the clouds were gathering out to sea and the sky was a leaden grey.

'You see,' Henry said, 'if the boat had been moored at the mouth of the creek we would have seen it, even on a day like yesterday. Visibility was bad, but not that poor early on. We just failed to look. Our focus was purely on the bodies and we didn't look past the end of our own noses.'

Constable Hargreaves looked uncomfortable. Mickey simply shrugged. 'What's done is done,' he said. 'We've got descriptions out all along the Medway and I've sent my negatives back with the bodies with instructions that pictures of these two should be circulated as widely as possible. As we discussed last night, the chances are they told us half-truths, so we know where we should be looking for them.'

'The only difficulty,' the constable said, 'would be that the boatmen look after one another. They watch out for each other's interests and can be close-mouthed when it comes to the authorities. It might take some time to track the little beggars down.'

Henry nodded. Everything that could be done was being done, he knew that, but it still rankled. 'Why here?' he said. 'We have to assume that at least part of the story is false. They could not have seen the bodies in the dark; they would not have been able to make them out, so . . .'

'Unless they were moored, and the bodies bumped up against the hull,' the constable suggested. 'As a lad I spent some time on the boats, the rivers, Medway and Thames, they're full of debris, full of floating obstacles. It's not uncommon to hear something hit the boat at night. You have to look to see what it is in case it fouls the anchor.'

'Unless that,' Henry agreed. 'But my gut is telling me otherwise. It's telling me that these men were killed, then held somewhere, probably in water, for a day or two. That this Garth and his boy were then charged with bringing them ashore and informing the authorities. Why this should be done I have as yet no idea, but my feeling is that it was done in such a way.'

'So, if you are right, the question is, as you say, why here? How many other places along this coast would have been a good site to dump bodies? Except,' Mickey continued, 'they weren't dumped, were they? They were brought here with the express intent of their being seen, and specifically seen here. Perhaps a message is being sent, after all. As we discussed last night, Bailey likes to display his dead; he likes his works to be known and to be recognized.'

'Though I've never known him to go to so much trouble,' Henry said.

For a little time the three of them prowled among the reeds, disturbing water birds and sinking their heels into the mud, but there was nothing to be seen and nothing to be found and nothing to be gained from remaining, so they headed back to the car and then to Cooper's farm.

Mrs Cooper welcomed them into a warm kitchen. Something that smelt of herbs and rabbit was cooking on the range and clothes hung to dry on a rack above the window.

They too would end up smelling of herbs and rabbit, Henry thought.

'My husband isn't here,' she told them, 'but I can tell you what went off yesterday.'

She sat them down with tea and cake and settled with them at the kitchen table, but Henry had the impression that they were interrupting her day and she'd like them gone. Ledgers lay open on the table top and she had apparently been dealing with the farm accounts.

She saw him looking. 'I have to keep the numbers straight,' she said. 'You don't keep your numbers up to date and you won't know where you are. I try to get them done once a week and I usually wait until Coops is away, otherwise he tries to help and then we're in a right pickle. We all have our strengths. This is one of mine.'

Henry nodded. 'My sister is the same,' he said. It was the first thing that came into his head and he wasn't sure it really applied, but the woman seemed satisfied by the remark.

'We'll not keep you long,' Mickey assured her. 'So, what happened yesterday?'

'Well.' She straightened her cup on the saucer. Imari pattern, Henry noticed absently. She'd brought out her best china for them. 'It was a little before eight o'clock and this man and boy came hammering at the door, telling us that they'd found bodies in the creek and would we call for the constable. They saw the telephone wires so they knew we had a phone here.'

'At about eight o'clock. You're sure of that?'

'I am. In fact it was a quarter to. The clock had just chimed. I told the man to wait up in the porch and then I telephoned to Constable Hargreaves. The man didn't want to bother with taking off his boots, and mired up to the elbows he was, so he wouldn't come inside – and I wasn't sorry about that, I can tell you.'

'And your husband was here?'

'Yes, he spoke to Hargreaves and was told that the constable would send a message and then come back to us, tell us if Coops would have to go with the cart. We both knew, you see, you'd not get a motor vehicle down that close. It would have to be horse and cart.'

'And then the man and boy left.'

'Yes. I gave them a bit of bread and dripping to take along and I'd given them mugs of hot tea while they waited, even if they didn't come in.' She paused. 'The porch is closed in, you know. They were out of the wind for a bit.'

'Mrs Cooper, what time did they leave?'

'Just after Coops had got off the phone. Just a bit after eight, I suppose it would be.'

She looked to Constable Hargreaves for confirmation.

'I was calling to London by a quarter past,' he said. 'We was all at the crime scene by noon. You did well to get down here so fast,' he commented, glancing at Henry and Mickey.

'We were lucky with the trains and lucky that you'd managed to arrange transport from the station,' Mickey told him.

Mrs Cooper was glancing anxiously at her housekeeping ledgers and there was nothing more anyone wanted to ask, so they departed soon after.

'So, they were at the farm by seven forty-five,' Henry commented as they returned to the car. 'How long would it take to walk here from the shoreline?'

'I'd say a good half an hour,' Hargreaves postulated.

'Which means they must have finished their task and had the bodies ashore by, say, seven o'clock, allowing for a few minutes to catch their breath? Another inconsistency in the story, I think. More and more I doubt there is any truth in it.'

* * *

Once back at the Crown, Henry announced his intention to head back to London, but asked that their rooms be kept available since they would undoubtedly return.

'There's no more we can do here,' Henry said as he and Mickey ate their lunch. Crusty bread and ham and pickle beside the fire. 'But it bothers me, Mickey. To pick a spot like this, inconvenient and far from anywhere, there must have been a reason for it. There is a narrative here that I can't read, but mark my words, there is history to it.'

1918

It had only been a few miles to Dalla's destination, but it felt like for ever, tramping the cold and snowy roads in the dark. The children were shivering and her own hands were blue despite the thick, hand-knitted mittens that she wore.

She was proud of her children. Kem and Malina made no complaints and only twice did Kem ask if they were almost there yet. It was some years since she'd been into the campsite on Ash Tree Lane in Gillingham, but she knew that it was still there, and that it still thrived and that she still had family among the people who lived there.

Despite what she had told her children, she was less confident about her welcome than she had sounded. She'd been gone for so long and, at Manfrid's insistence, had largely cut ties and even while he'd been away at the Front, her fear of him had been such that she had not completely gone against his directions. Her mother and sisters had written a few times, her sister Sarah being the scribe for the family because she had the best hand, and Dalla had written back. On one occasion she had talked about Manfrid's violence, but she had been careful what she said. Manfrid, for all that he had wanted to break contact with his past, was also still kin. There were many who would not take kindly to her speaking out against a husband who had been chosen for her, though she had married him gladly enough. Time was when she'd been taken in by the glamour of him, darkly handsome and a renowned bare-knuckle fighter, and she'd not looked further than that.

Dalla hoped that Malina would be wiser in her choices than she herself had been.

It was two in the morning by the time they arrived and all three were chilled to the bone. Malina stood with her hand on the five-bar gate and looked askance at her mother. 'We came here before, when I was just a little thing. Have we arrived, then?'

Dalla nodded and Malina unhooked the latch and the three of them entered the camp. Dalla felt an unexpected sense of relief. Whatever people might think, whatever they might say and whatever Dalla might be answerable for would wait till morning. No one would turn them away on a night like this.

The caravans and cabins were dark for the most part, and no one was obviously on watch, but she was not surprised when, after a moment or two, a man stepped out of the shadows and asked what their business was. He held a lantern and shone it on their faces, and she identified herself and told the man that these were her children and that she was looking for 'Tan Fuller. 'He's my uncle. His wife is Lizzie, and she's my mother's sister. I don't think me mam's here, but she's Annie Cooper.'

The man studied them for a little longer and then he turned on his heel and beckoned them to follow. He led them between rows of vans and then knocked on a door. Lights showed and the door opened and Dalla breathed real relief. 'Sarah! My God, Sarah, I couldn't be happier.'

Her sister stared at her and then stared at the children, and then she opened her door wide. 'What the 'eck are you lot doing out, night like this? And where is your man? Is he not with you?'

Dalla urged the children up the steps and into the caravan. 'He's dead,' she said. 'Crossed the wrong man once too often and they had him killed. I don't know no more than that. Men came in, they just told us to go, burned our cottage down.'

The man who had escorted them shifted restlessly. 'All well, is it, Sarah?'

'Reckon it is,' she said. She closed the door and they all stood uncertainly in the tiny space. Sarah pulled her shawl tightly around her shoulders and shivered. 'You look frozen 'alf to death,' she said. 'We'll find you somewhere to bed down for the night and then in the morning we'll talk about this. You'll have to explain yourself, you know that. The old people will want to know.'

Dalla nodded. That was to be expected, but she was more certain of her welcome now. Sarah was well respected, well on the way to being a matriarch in her own right, and women were listened to, where women and children were concerned.

'Is Ma here?' she asked.

'Not yet. She's not been well, so they're takin' the journey slow. Another few days and she will be. She's missed you, Dalina, we all have.'

Dalina. It was a long time since anyone had called her that. Dalla felt that she wanted to cry.

Sarah and her eldest bustled round and sorted out sleeping spaces. Dalla would sleep with her sister and the children were tucked in beside Sarah's own. It was cramped, but it was warm and that was all that mattered right now.

'I always thought it would be you that did for Manfrid,' Sarah said as they settled down to sleep. 'I'm glad it wasn't. I'd never want to see you hang, not for the likes of him.'

Sarah, she remembered, had tried to talk her out of the marriage. But Dalla had been fifteen – and rather stupid, in retrospect. Flattered by the attentions of this much older man who promised her the earth and delivered nothing. Sarah leaned over and kissed her sister on the forehead, just as she often had when they were both children and she, as the eldest, was left in charge. 'Go to sleep,' she said. 'There's nothing so dark it can't be solved by daylight.'

FIVE

1928

Henry Johnstone had returned to London with Mickey that afternoon, and evening found him back in his own flat. His sister, Cynthia, telephoned and suggested he come for the weekend. She and her husband were having a house party and she would love him to be there.

Henry smiled. 'And how many of your friends will be offering me jobs?' he asked. It was a standing joke between them that Cynthia thought he should be something other than a policeman. Something that didn't involve so many dead bodies, but she knew he would not leave his job and he knew that she would not quite give up on trying to make life 'better' for him. Even now she still played the Big Sister role.

'I'll try and come on Sunday,' he said. 'It would be good to see you all, and Melissa and I must arrange another shopping trip.' Melissa was her middle child, wedged between two boys; she was serious and bright and loved books and Henry regularly took her out on trips. He tried to be even handed and arrange treats for the boys too, but his only success so far had been the occasional cricket match. The truth was, the boys preferred the company of his sergeant, Mickey. Mickey talked about sport and boxing and aeroplanes and photography, and although Henry was interested in all of those things, he recognized he did not have Mickey Hitchens' natural ability to communicate that interest.

The truth was, although Henry loved his sister's children deeply, he did find children in general a little difficult. Melissa was something of an exception.

'Melissa will love that,' Cynthia said. 'Do try to come, Henry. It's been weeks since we last had a catch-up.'

Henry assured her that he'd do his best, that he would try and get away for a few hours at least.

He replaced the receiver and went to sit in his favourite chair looking out over the river and wondered if he would actually manage it. On returning to London, Mickey had taken his remaining film for processing and the fingerprints he had lifted after the break-in at the Crown for inspection and comparison. Henry had been involved in compiling a list of known associates of Bailey and his people. There would be raids the following morning, bright and early, before anybody was awake. The press had not yet got hold of the story, the area was so remote and the bodies not yet publicly identified, and so the central office at Scotland Yard felt it still had the element of surprise on its side.

Henry had expressed his niggling feeling that the scene had been set up in some way, that there was planning behind it and that more people than they expected might know about the death of Billy Crane and whoever the other man might turn out to be. If he was a known associate, then the likelihood of quick identification was high, there would be a mug shot of him somewhere in the files.

Henry watched the traffic on the river and wondered where the man and boy had fetched up. How deep in this mess were they? Or was it just that they'd been paid to dump the bodies on the shore?

He fetched his journal from the pocket of his coat and sat down, pen in hand, trying to gather his thoughts.

> *There is history to this*, he wrote. *I sense it, something deeper and older than a recent argument between Josiah Bailey and his men. I can't shake the feeling that a message is being sent but who that message might be for is another matter. A message to the police would be writ more plainly. I think this is something that only a handful of people might understand and until we find out who they might be, we might make no headway with this.*

He laid his book aside and reached for the photographs that he'd brought home with him, the shots that Mickey had taken on the mud flats. He studied them again, looking at the faces of man and boy, the constables working, the bodies lying on the foreshore at the markers which the constable had told him delineated the reach of high and low tide and, visible in the distance, the wooden wharves that boats tied up to for loading and unloading in the creek.

There were no boats visible close by apart from the small rowing boat that had been used to tow the bodies ashore. The man and boy were unremarkable, in their work clothes. The man wore a heavy jersey and, Henry guessed, multiple layers beneath. The boy a similar jersey beneath what had once been a good quality Norfolk jacket, now much mended. He had a scarf wrapped around his neck and a knitted hat pulled down over his ears. Mickey had guessed he was about twelve, but he looked small and wiry and could have been two or three years either side of that.

The names they had given were Frederick and Eddy Garth, Eddy being the boy. It was too much to hope that they were genuine and yet they seemed unusual enough to have the ring of authenticity.

'Garth is hardly a common name,' Henry mused. 'If you make up a name, surely it would be easier to think of a Smith or a Jones or a Brown, so perhaps they know someone called Garth. And I would make a bet that they kept their own first names. The lie that's hard to keep track of is the one most likely to be exposed.'

He made a note of this in his journal, and then decided that he would try and sleep. He'd had eight nights now of not sleeping, of restless dreams and tossing and turning, but this particular anniversary was almost past now and he hoped he might be free for a little while and not dream of men shouting warnings, and the gas cloud coming, and others choking to death as their own blood filled their lungs.

The following morning was surprisingly bright. The rain had cleared and a brisk wind was drying the streets. He'd remembered to brush his coat; it had taken considerable and vigorous application of the clothes brush to get rid of the river mud.

The central office was buzzing with activity when he got there. A dozen arrests had been made, men and women had been brought in for questioning and interviews had already commenced. Mickey showed him the list and Henry recognized most of the names on it. 'I think I'll start with Thomas Boswell,' he said. 'Unless he's already been taken through.'

Mickey checked the interview list and shook his head. 'No, he's still in a holding cell. Any particular reason?'

'Tommy Boswell and I have met before. I know him to be a nervous sort, more thoughtful than most too. It's possible we may be able to apply some leverage.'

Mickey nodded. 'I've already spoken with Matilda Carthy. She is, as usual, busy saying she's not going to speak to anyone and her brother, Ian, is listing all the things he didn't do in the last six months, by which we might assume he was involved in every single one of them.'

Henry smiled. They'd met both of the Carthys before, and their other siblings, and this was their normal reaction. The sister had served time for receiving stolen goods. Most of the brothers had housebreaking experience. Ian was the only one who had actually not been inside – not through want of trying, on the part of the police, but through want of solid evidence. The Carthys did odd jobs for Bailey but were not part of the inner circle.

'See what shakes loose,' he said. 'In the past we've been known to pick up odds and sods of useful information from what Ian *doesn't* tell us. I'll go and see how things lie with Thomas Boswell. Any news on identification? The man and boy, or the other body?'

Mickey shook his head. 'Nothing so far. We've shown pictures to everyone we brought in and we've compared mug shots, but our second body still seems to be something of a mystery. If he has a record, then it's not with us, though of course the Kent Constabulary might turn up something. As to the mysterious Garths, father and son or whatever they are, there's been no word as yet.'

Henry nodded. Descriptions and now photographs had been distributed but he expected no quick response, especially among a community that was both inherently mobile and inevitably close and protective.

Henry was inclined to think that the Garths, or whatever their proper names might be, were the smaller part of this puzzle.

'The post-mortem examinations have been scheduled for tomorrow morning,' Mickey added. 'They will begin promptly at nine.'

'Good,' Henry approved. 'So, for now, we see what Mr Thomas Boswell has to say for himself.'

Tommy Boswell was a small man. Five feet three and wiry rather than muscular. He was, according to his sheet, thirty-five years old but he looked older. Older, Henry thought, and world-weary.

A pack of cigarettes and a book of matches lay on the rough wooden table and Tommy fiddled with them as he spoke, as though he'd like to light up but wasn't sure if that was either allowed or advisable. Henry didn't think that Tommy was particularly in awe of his surroundings or of his having been hauled in at the crack of dawn by a cohort of burly constables. Tommy Boswell was simply a cautious and wary man, a lesson in life learned early and observed ever since.

He looked at the photographs Henry had set before him. Two dead men, dressed in sodden clothes and lying on saturated ground.

'Recognize them?' Henry asked.

Tommy's gaze flicked from the photographs to Henry and then back again. His hands were still occupied with the cigarettes and book of matches. He smoked Player's, Henry noted, a common enough brand, though he had half expected Tommy to have smoked roll-ups. The matchbook bore the name of a hotel, the Esplanade, that Henry didn't recognize. He noted it down. It didn't sound like London.

'Recognize them?' Henry asked again.

'Billy Crane,' Tommy dabbed a finger at the left-hand body.

'And the other?'

Tommy shrugged. 'Hard to tell, his face is muddy, like. Could be anyone.'

'One of Bailey's men?'

Tommy shrugged again. 'How would I know?'

'You work for Josiah Bailey. You worked for his father.'

'You live where I live, who doesn't, one way or another.'

'And this man?'

'I told you, I don't recognize him.' He paused, his hands becoming still, and leaned forward a little, studying Henry. 'I'm just an errand boy. An odd job man. Bailey wants something done and there's no one better, I do it for him. End of story. I'm no Billy Crane.'

'Billy was close to Bailey.'

Tommy leaned back in his chair and picked up the matchbook, twirled it between his fingers. 'Billy was a favoured child,' he said. 'Bailey used him often enough. He'll not be happy.'

'Unless he was the one who ordered the killing?'

Tommy looked up in what Henry could see was genuine surprise.

'No? He's done it before.'

'So you say. He's served no time for killing, has he? Never come close to feeling the rope, has he?'

'But you don't think this is his handiwork. You were shocked by the idea. Why is that, Tommy? Why would Bailey not arrange the death of Billy Crane?'

'I told you, he was a favoured child.'

'Bailey's child.'

Tommy shrugged. 'How would I know that?'

'Bailey's known to have had relationships with a number of women.'

'What man hasn't? It's a wise man that knows his own father, isn't that what they say?'

Henry paused and then changed tack. He slid another photograph across the table, that of the man and boy.

Tommy looked at it and then shrugged his shoulders again. 'Sailorman and a boy,' he said. 'What about them?'

'How long have you known Billy Crane?'

Tommy made as if to shrug again and then changed his mind and frowned instead. 'Grew up together. We was more or less the same age, lived in the same street, knew one another for always. Like I said, you live where I live you work for the Baileys one way or another, even if you don't know that's what you're doing. There's not an errand boy in the next ten streets who doesn't run an errand for the family, sooner or later, or a tradesman doesn't pay dues, or a woman – well, you know. He doesn't touch the married ones, though, you got to give him that.'

Henry didn't think he had to give Josiah Bailey anything. 'And Bailey senior, I've heard he's fading fast, that he has little to do with anything these days.'

'Not seen the old man in a long time.'

'You think he's dead?'

'I think they'll have the funeral when it suits them,' Tommy said. And then, as though he thought he'd said too much, clamped his lips tight and returned his gaze to the cigarette packet on the table.

'And your relationship with Billy Crane?'

'He was there, I was there, we did this and that. We were not *friends*, if that's what you mean. Just two people in the same place at the same time.'

Henry said nothing and Tommy shifted restlessly in his seat. 'Nothing I can tell you. Bailey won't be pleased, though.'

'Not pleased at losing his favoured child,' Henry said. 'But I wouldn't have thought that would bother you, Tommy, seeing as how he's no longer around. Seeing as how none of you seem to know where he is, seeing as how he's been on the run since last autumn. Why would it bother you that Bailey might be displeased?'

'I never said it did.' He shifted restlessly again and this time opened the pack of cigarettes and removed one, tapped it on the carton but still hesitated about lighting up.

'Go ahead,' Henry told him. 'You may smoke.'

Tommy scowled and put the cigarette away, then moved both hands clear of the packet, as though the temptation might be too much. Instead, he tapped the fingers of both hands in a broken rhythm on the cracked top of the wooden table, pausing only to pick at splinters with the tip of a broken and dirty nail.

Henry watched him, saying nothing and letting the silence lengthen, allowing Tommy's nerves to do his work for him. Eventually he asked, 'I don't suppose you have any views on where Bailey might have gone to.' It was not really a question, simply a statement of the fact that Tommy was in the know but would not talk, and Henry voiced it only because it was expected of him.

Henry got up, paced the room. Less than six steps long each way. He moved behind Tommy and the man flinched as though expecting an attack, but Henry merely passed him and then returned to his seat. 'Both men were stabbed,' he said. 'No doubt you will be reporting back to someone, if not to Bailey himself, so you can tell whoever you plan to tell that both men were stabbed. At close quarters, facing their assailants at the time of their deaths, but it's likely that their hands were bound and they were unable to defend themselves. It's also likely that there were two assailants; the weapons were different.' Henry was guessing here, but he watched Tommy's reaction closely. Tommy Boswell's face was guarded and closed, that wariness very evident now.

'Then they were dumped in water, left for a day or two before being dragged ashore by the boatman and his boy. We don't know what part, if any, they had to play, apart from bringing the bodies in and summoning help, so they'd be noticed and found. Someone certainly wanted them found. It would have been easy to have made them disappear, don't you think, Tommy? So it seems to me that perhaps, Billy Crane being this favoured child and all that, someone is sending a message to Josiah Bailey, telling him perhaps that his days are numbered? Or would you read it differently?'

He had Tommy Boswell's attention now. His eyes were still focused on Henry's face.

'It seemed like a strange place to find the bodies,' Henry said. 'Isolated, in the middle of nowhere. Odd, don't you think?'

Tommy clearly didn't want to ask the next question, but he couldn't help himself, and that intrigued Henry. 'Where was they found?'

'A place called Otterham Creek, near the village of Upchurch. Do you know it?'

Tommy Boswell shook his head, but Henry could see that his face had paled and his lips were tight. One hand now gripped the cigarette packet and the other was clenched into a fist.

'You look upset, Tommy,' Henry said. 'Perhaps you were

closer to Billy Crane than you let on. Perhaps he was a friend of yours, after all. Or perhaps you both had business near that village of Upchurch?'

'Never been there.' Tommy shook his head vehemently.

'It seems a little off the beaten track, I suppose. But we've heard that Josiah Bailey's family have connections in the area. That they have family thereabouts. Have you heard that, Tommy?'

Tommy Boswell had relaxed, just a little, Henry noticed. So this wasn't about *Bailey's* family; so Henry's strikes were wide of the mark, as yet.

'Billy Crane upset someone from down there? Stabbing is a personal thing: up close, you get to look into the eyes of the man you are killing. Takes a certain nerve, a certain steel, don't you think?'

Tommy had lost interest now, Henry could see that. But there had been a reaction. Something Henry had said had briefly upset the man he'd been questioning. He was right: there was history here, but how far back?

'You both served, you and Crane. You were at the Front.'

'We did our bit. You suggesting that we didn't? Bailey senior demanded it anyhow, said we were fighting for King and country, all his men did their bit.'

'Not that there was much option,' Henry reminded him. 'I don't expect you *volunteered* until conscription was in . . .'

He paused, noting the look of anger and frustration cross the other man's face, and Henry waited to be told that he was wrong. That Thomas Boswell had been proud to sign up, right from the start, though he must have waited until late in 1914, Henry thought, before the height restrictions were dropped from five feet six back to five feet three. Tommy would only just have made that height.

Unless he'd joined one of the bantam regiments, of course . . .

Henry allowed his mind to play with the problem for a moment, waiting for Tommy to speak. But Tommy said nothing.

'Of course,' Henry proceeded, 'Bailey would have been less worried that someone might come muscling in on his territories with the hard men of all colours being called away. Boys and old men can only do so much when they are all that is left behind. Did you and Crane serve together?'

Tommy nodded. 'East Surreys. Same division.'

'Which would have brought you closer, I would imagine?'

Again, that physical reaction. That tightening of hands and mouth. '*Not* closer, then. Perhaps it had the opposite effect. Perhaps you saw Crane as he was and didn't like what you saw.'

'What does that have to do with anything?'

'Perhaps you're not sorry to see Billy Crane dead. Perhaps the only thing you're sorry for is that you were not the man holding the knife.'

'And how do you know it wasn't me?' Tommy laughed shortly. 'You think I don't have the stomach for it, is that it? We all killed in the war.'

'War is different,' Henry said sharply. 'Well, did you do it?' He waited. 'No, I thought not.'

Henry got to his feet again and leaned across the table and Tommy, reflecting the movement, leaned back in his chair and looked up into Henry's face.

'I have a hunch,' Henry said, 'that whoever did this will not be satisfied with just Billy Crane and whoever this other man might be. Bailey has left a vacuum, simply by not being in his usual place, by not ruling his usual streets. So who is moving in, Tommy? Who is looking to take over from Josiah Bailey and his family? And how many are they likely to kill in getting there?'

There was no reaction. This time, no physical tell or tic, so this was not something that worried Thomas Boswell, even if it was possibly true. Tommy was just an errand boy, as he said; a random foot soldier who could just as soon serve one man as another, who was adapted to life in the same place, whoever happened to be in temporary charge. So what was bothering him? Henry wondered. He was annoyed by the fact that he'd obviously touched a nerve on several occasions, and yet he'd not been able to push that advantage forward.

He straightened up, instinct and experience telling him that he was going to gain nothing more from continuing the interview, that more was likely to be gained by letting Tommy

Boswell go and, if possible, having him observed – though men like Boswell were slippery as eels and disappeared as quickly in the streets of London as eels did in the reed beds. He knew that Tommy Boswell would go straight to Josiah Bailey with his report, or would report to someone who would then pass his words on, and he fervently wished that he could observe Bailey's reaction when they were delivered.

Without another word Henry turned and went out, deliberately leaving the photographs on the table. He would give orders that Tommy Boswell was to be kept there for half an hour or so and then told he could go, and in the meantime Henry put what observation he could in place, ready for his release.

It was late in the afternoon by the time the interviews were completed and all but a handful of those brought in had been sent on their way. There had been a number of almost by-blow confessions made during the course of the day; for some, less experienced and less self-assured, the simple fact of being woken before dawn and dragged into a police cell, then interviewed by a couple of burly detectives, had been enough to elicit a confession – in a couple of cases to crimes the police didn't even have on their books.

But nothing pertinent to their current inquiry had emerged. Henry was relatively unperturbed by this. In part, the actions of the day had been designed to send shockwaves in Bailey's direction; it would have been too much to expect that it would bring a solution.

Henry sat down at his accustomed desk in the central office and shuffled through his notes. The place was quiet now, a handful of detectives, similarly employed. He glanced up at the 'board' and noticed that, as he and Mickey were currently logged for an investigation, their names had been moved down. Chief Inspector Savage was currently first on the board, on immediate call, should a murder shout come in. Bag packed and he and his sergeant ready to respond.

It was largely due to a high-profile investigation that Savage had headed up that detectives now had their 'murder bag'. A pack of essential items for the observation and collection of evidence, including pairs of rubber gloves (the previous practice had been to handle bodies without any such basic protection). It was after the pathologist, Bernard Spilsbury, had arrived at a crime scene in Pevensey Bay and found Savage and his men handling putrefying flesh with their bare hands that he and senior officers had decided something should be done.

Mickey was currently restocking their own kit and adding the extra film and chemicals that Henry had decided they should carry.

Second on the board was Chief Inspector George Cornish, who only the previous year had made headlines by solving the murder of Minnie Bonati, whose dismembered body had been found in a trunk in Charing Cross.

Third on the list was Prothero.

Henry still sometimes found it strange that he should be working in such illustrious company.

He closed his eyes and stretched back in his chair, trying to pull the knots and kinks out of his back. He opened them again on hearing something being dumped down on to his table. Mickey stood there, newly stocked bag set before him.

'They lost Tommy Boswell in one of the alleys off Brick Lane,' Mickey told him.

'No surprise. He's well practised in being invisible. Revealing, though, I think.'

Mickey grabbed a chair and plonked down on the other side of the desk. 'How so?'

'He'd be aware that we'd keep him under observation. If he simply wanted to pass information along, he'd have met one of Bailey's other associates in a local pub. One way or another, anything he had to report would have filtered back to Bailey. Tommy himself would have remained in plain sight.'

'The fact that he took the trouble to shake off his followers suggests he wanted to see Bailey and report direct.' Mickey nodded. 'Though that's attributing some capacity for subtle thought to our friend Tommy.'

'True, but as you say, he's spent a lifetime being invisible and unconsidered. He could be said to have made a career of it. That's how he's survived – both Bailey and his fits of temper and the hazards of being useful to Bailey. My guess is that the man himself is now back in London.'

'Which probably doesn't help us one iota,' Mickey observed. 'Bailey's mob is tight and we could schedule raids on likely places between here and Christmas and still miss him.'

'But his grip isn't as tight as it used to be. Sooner or later he'll slip up or someone else will. Anyway . . .' Henry stood up and stretched again. Sure sign, Mickey knew, that he was fatigued and hungry.

'Food,' Mickey said. 'And a beer. Come on, let's be having you. One small piece of good news: we now have a couple of names attached to our mystery body. One person recognized him as the elder brother of Sonny Peterson, now deceased. Remember him? Housebreaking, robbery with violence, threats to kill, until somebody finally threatened *him* and then did it. Never one of Bailey's crew, so far as we know.'

'Interesting,' Henry said as he collected his coat. 'But no first name for this brother?'

'Well, another of today's guests suggested his name might be Max and also thought he might be related to Sonny, so I'm thinking—'

'That putting those two fragments together would give us a Max Peterson. And does this Max Peterson have a record?'

'Surprisingly not, given the company he's probably kept – always supposing that's who he is, of course. Clean as a whistle, at least in our records. We sent a call out to Kent Constabulary, seeing as that's where his body was found, and will spread the net wider if necessary, but a *lack* of record, in my book, is suspicious enough. Sonny Peterson had one long as your arm, and the younger brother, Alf Peterson, is serving time. Armed robbery, and a man died. He was a juvenile at the time so got off with a life term; his two colleagues got their necks stretched.'

'So we show him the picture of his possible brother.'

'Already in hand,' Mickey said. 'Now, beer and food, probably in that order, and then we get ourselves some sleep. How's that working for you, by the way?'

'Somewhat better, last night.'

'Better by your standards or better by normal standards?'

Henry just smiled. 'Cynthia phoned. I'm going to try and get over to hers on Sunday. Apparently she's having a house party over the weekend, but it will be good to see her anyway.'

'Give her my best. I'm expecting a weekend of domestic bliss,' Mickey said, with only a little irony.

'Belle is home, then?'

'She is indeed. The tour has finished and she should be back in town for at least a few weeks.' He sounded very content with the idea. Mickey and his wife had a somewhat unconventional marriage, which hadn't done him any good in the promotion stakes and meant that Henry had sometimes had to defend his sergeant from those who considered he was not living quite as proper and upright a life as they would expect. Henry liked Belle; she was an independent woman who had refused to give up her independence just because she happened to fall in love and get married. And frankly, Henry couldn't see why she ought to have done. But then, Henry had been largely raised by his sister Cynthia. And, he was content to acknowledge, this probably skewed his view of such things.

SIX

Josiah Bailey was watching two men sparring. Both were young, juveniles not yet tested in the professional ring, but they showed promise. One had black skin and his father worked as a stevedore in the docks, the other was white and pale, though his fluffy blond hair was currently darkened by sweat and slicked back. He was the son of one of Bailey's long-term associates. Bailey had decided that both were worth his time and every few days, when opportunity allowed, he took his place alongside their trainer and watched them work.

The boxing gym was in the basement of a warehouse. It had been there more than twenty years and produced some good fighters, though not all of them had gone out on to the public circuit. Betting men did not always like to bet in public and not all of his fighters could show their face where a police officer might see it, so two worlds occupied this one space and Bailey was king of both, even now.

Word had filtered back all day about the raids and the police interviews and Bailey was annoyed about Billy Crane. He'd been a good lad, had Billy. Maybe not too bright, but loyal and capable where it counted. He could make a guess as to who the other man might have been; Billy Crane and Max Peterson were practically inseparable and had been so for as long as Bailey could remember. Close – some said too close and Bailey should intervene, hinting at a kind of closeness that many said was sinful. Bailey chose not to know about that sort of thing, not where useful men were concerned, so long as they kept it quiet and made enough of a show with the women for talk to remain only talk (and even that was in hushed tones, and not where anyone that mattered could hear it).

He was perfectly aware of what Billy and Max were, and were to one another, but they had never tipped the balance and been *less* than useful, or *less* than loyal, and so he had chosen not to make an issue or an example. They knew how to keep everything within bounds and behind closed doors.

Thomas Boswell was the first actually to come and report to him in person and he now sat uncomfortably perched on a wooden chair on the left-hand side of Bailey. Bailey, eyes fixed on the two young men circling in the ring, had barely acknowledged Tommy's presence, a slight inclination of the head was all. He'd felt no need to ask Tommy about his having been followed. It was inevitable that the police would have trailed him and just as inevitable that Tommy would have shaken them off before coming here. Anything less and Tommy would not have survived Bailey's anger, and he knew that.

'Stabbed, you say.'

'Two different hands. I don't know how they know that, but the copper reckoned there were two different weapons used. Max and Billy both had their hands tied, they couldn't defend themselves. Then they put them in water, left them, and then got this man and boy to drag them onshore.' He paused. 'I brought pictures. The copper, he must have forgot to pick them up when he left the room, so I slipped them in me pocket.'

'I doubt he forgot,' Bailey said. 'Give them to me.'

He could see that Tommy's hands were shaking as he held out the two small images.

Bailey studied them closely. 'And where did you say this was? Where they fetched up?'

Tommy shrugged, as though the name meant nothing to him. 'Some village called Upchurch,' he said. 'Water somewhere near, a creek or some such, something to do with otters . . . Otterham, I think he said.'

Bailey frowned. Vague memories surfaced, but he couldn't quite place them as yet. Something had happened out that way. A lot of years ago. It would come to him . . . Ah, that was right.

For the first time he turned to look directly at Tommy Boswell. 'You've been there,' he said. 'Within a mile or two. Ten-year back. You fetched the Beaney woman and her kids away, when we did her old man. A liar and a traitor he was, so I had an example made of him. Maxie wasn't there, but you were. You and Billy, you went to fetch the woman and the children. Senior gave them money, told them to skedaddle. So, from what I remember, you put them on a train, burned the cottage to the ground.'

Tommy's jaw dropped. 'Manfrid Beaney? Wife was Dalina. You think . . .'

'I think nothing,' Bailey said. 'Not if you put them on a train and they went, like sensible people. Word was Dalla Beaney *was* a sensible woman and went quietly, or so I was led to believe.'

Tommy nodded his head violently. 'That's what I heard too. And that's what happened. She didn't say nothing, just took her kids and their few bits they had and went.'

'So, no trouble there, then. Must be something else, then, mustn't it?'

Tommy felt himself dismissed, so he got up and backed away. 'They left,' he said. 'I saw them go. Dalla, she had too much sense to come back.'

Bailey turned to look at him again, his eyes cold and expressionless. 'But the kids will be all grown up now, won't they?'

Tommy absorbed what he was saying. 'They had no love for their dad. Violent bugger he was, made their lives hell.'

'I hope you're right, Tommy boy.'

Tommy nodded. He hoped he was right too.

SEVEN

1925

The transfer of Ricky Clough to Durham gaol was to take place on the morning of November twenty-third and it was unlikely that any tears would be shed the day the man finally went.

Clough, the governor thought, was an inveterate trouble-maker. When he'd first arrived he'd gathered around him a clique of those who considered themselves hard men, but as time went on even this coterie had fallen off and found other alliances – though if Clough said jump, they would still ask how high. He'd been put in solitary, he'd been put in a shared cell with two others of similar reputation, he'd been given a single cell, he'd been singled out for discipline . . . nothing worked with the man the governor was convinced would have ended up hanged, if he'd just been given a little more rope on the outside.

And a good thing that would have been. Eventually, after his continuing complaints, it had been agreed that Clough would be transferred to a maximum-security facility and, Durham being the closest option, that was where he would be heading.

A van with driver, two armed guards and the prisoner in chains set off on what was an impressively bright morning for so late in the year. Clough was solid rather than large. Barrel chested, and with unusual strength in his arms. Last time he'd attacked a fellow inmate it had taken four officers, with batons, to get him to let go. Bleeding from the head and with a broken arm, Clough had still refused to give in.

The governor personally checked his shackles, clamped down tight so he could reach neither of the accompanying guards, and sent the armoured van on its way with a sense of relief. It was relief which would be only short-lived.

Six miles out of Durham, on a narrow road taken because it offered a direct and swift route, the van driver spotted an accident. He shouted back to the men in the body of the van.

'Looks like a cart gone over. There's a horse on its side, still in the traces, and it's blocking our way. I'm going to have to pull in.'

'Turn around and head the other way,' came the rather tense response.

'And what if someone's hurt?'

'And we do what if they are, put them in the back with this bastard? Turn round and we'll sound the alarm at that village we passed through back there.'

The van slowed and the driver, grumbling that he didn't like it one bit, began to turn. Then a shot rang out and he slumped forward against the wheel.

'Charlie, what the hell's going on . . . Charlie?'

No answer from the driver. The engine still running, the sound of someone bashing hard against the rear doors. Clough sat up, suddenly interested.

'Fucking hell.' The van doors swung open and three armed men stood in the road beyond. One guard fired; was dead before the bullet left the gun.

'Keys.' The man had a cloth muffling the lower half of his face.

Keys were handed over. Clough was released and beckoned from the van. The second guard, relieved of his gun, sat with hands raised, staring in terror at the men who had broken his prisoner free.

'Out,' the masked man told him.

Clough turned as the guard stepped down from the van. No one expected what happened next. He seized hold of the guard, held him high above his head and then sent him crashing to the ground.

'What the hell did you do that for? He was doing what we told him.'

Clough shrugged. 'And so what?' he said. 'Now, tell me. Just who the fuck are you?'

EIGHT

1928; Saturday

At nine o'clock on the Saturday morning Henry and Mickey stood in the cold basement of Bart's Hospital watching Taylor, the pathologist, as he minutely examined the body of Billy Crane. Taylor, as frequently happened in Mickey's experience, had arrived early that morning and had already dealt with Max Peterson. The report slip for Peterson's body already lay on the bench set to one side of the examination room.

The conclusion on Peterson's report was unsurprising. Death from a single stab wound that had penetrated from beneath the ribs, perforated the diaphragm and plunged into the heart. Angle of the blow had been upward and the weapon had a blade of perhaps an inch and a half wide and five or six inches long.

The weapon that had killed Billy Crane was a little more unusual. Taylor's best guess was that it was some kind of conical spike perhaps two inches in diameter at its widest point. The angle of that blow was different too, entering between the ribs, but again penetrating lung and heart.

The deaths of both men must have been pretty instantaneous.

'You notice that the hands of both were bound,' Taylor said. 'What you probably didn't have leisure to notice was that they had also been bound at the feet. My guess is that they were weighted down and left in the water for a time. Not that they would have floated yet, of course. In summer I would expect them to become floaters after five or six days, but this time of year in the cold water, it could take anything up to a couple of weeks. Fermentation within the gut being slower, of course, than it would have been in warm weather. But whoever did for this pair wanted to make sure they stayed down, presumably until it suited their purpose to move them.'

He pointed to the ligature marks on Billy Crane's ankles. The ropes had cut deep into the flesh and pulled down at a slight angle, indicating that something had been dragging against them. Henry nodded; that fitted with what they had suspected.

Mickey shifted restlessly, foot to foot. He had no objection to watching such medical dismemberment but was sometimes irritated by both the length of time the operation took and the chilly environment in which it took place. He was deeply interested in the ways in which photography, science and proper observation assisted in their work, but he was also, at heart, much more of a 'tramping the streets' and 'knocking on doors' sort of officer. Knowing people, knowing where and how they lived and the pressures and impulses that led them to commit their crimes was what interested him.

Henry was of a somewhat opposing persuasion. His habit of attending post-mortems (and bringing Mickey along) was one at which colleagues often looked askance.

'How long were they in the water?' Henry asked, dragging his heavy coat more tightly across his chest. 'We thought perhaps a day or two?'

Taylor nodded briefly. 'Both were dead when they entered the water. Neither had eaten for perhaps twelve hours or more prior to death. Stomachs were empty. None of the usual signs of drowning. No water in the lungs or foaming in the trachea or about the mouth. No, these two were dead before that.'

Mickey sighed. He knew that Henry was trying to speed the process; knew also that Taylor was not a man to be hurried. He liked to tell his story at his own speed, in his own way, as if ticking off a list. He supposed they were fortunate that it wasn't Spilsbury taking the post-mortems. The great Bernard Spilsbury was quick, efficient and totally against any observation of his work, eschewing even the services of a note-taker or secretary. He even posted his report slips himself.

Mickey, for all the tedium, was in agreement with his inspector that it was better to see the process, to understand it, to gain knowledge of it.

He shifted his weight again, allowed his gaze to drift about the tiled walls, the small high windows of the basement lab, the naked bulbs on long, twisted cords.

'Fleas,' Taylor said unexpectedly. 'Fortunately for us, both of your men had them.'

'Fleas?' Henry was as puzzled as his sergeant.

'In those little sample dishes, over on that bench. Lively little pests.'

Henry crossed to the bench and picked up the sample bottle. 'Fleas,' he said. 'I'm not sure I understand.'

'Human fleas are strange creatures. Fortunately for us they can survive a little immersion in water. A human flea will typically drown within thirty hours of submersion, sometimes more quickly. I found our little friends there in the armpits of both men, combed them out and put them into a bottle and left them for a while. It took them a few hours to dry out and start moving again, by which I deduce that they had been in the water for upwards of a day, but certainly not for as much as two. Not all of the fleas revived, of course, but as you can see, four or five little blighters made it through. So unless there are particularly virulent and hardy strains of human flea in the population of East London, I would place the upper time of their immersion at perhaps thirty hours. Certainly no more and probably closer to a single day.'

'They must have been held somewhere and then transported to where we found them,' Henry said. 'There is no way of telling where they might first have gone into the water.'

Taylor shook his head. 'But my guess would be fresh water rather than brine. There are injuries to the bodies, *post mortem*, as though moving water has bashed them against a wall or a boat keel or something of the sort, and of course there is some animal damage, but my *personal* opinion is that in brine I would have expected more damage from crabs and other nibblers. As I say, it is only a guess.'

Henry thanked him and they left soon after. It was ten in the morning and the weather was reasonably bright. Henry, Mickey had noticed, had become very suspicious of the weather this winter, on the watch for snow. The January of 1928 had been a difficult one. Heavy snow followed by a sudden thaw in the first week had led to flooding and the Thames had broken its banks. Fourteen people had died and many thousands were made homeless and, if Mickey remembered right, there had been another death. A woman, a known prostitute, had been killed, not by the Thames, but by a stab wound strangely like that which had taken the life of Max Peterson.

Mickey said, 'The shape of the wound—'

'Is similar to the one we found on Martha Howells' body. Yes. And it's unusual enough to suppose that the two are possibly linked.'

'Martha Howells' world was one of prostitutes and punters.'

'And we still have no criminal record for Max Peterson.' Henry nodded thoughtfully. 'Mickey, there is little more to be done today. Go home to Belle and give her my best wishes and regards.'

Only a few streets away, a man was running. His pursuers chased him down Commercial Road, through Saturday morning crowds. People paid very little attention to the man running and the two behind. Looking at the faces of all three, most considered it wiser not to see.

The running man did not dare stop and ask for help. He knew he wouldn't get it anyway. The men chased him into Myrdle Street and he dodged down an alleyway between two buildings and into the yard at the back of Willacy's General Stores and Chophouse, grabbed the wall beyond and tried to swing over, but they were on him now. They never said a word, silent and efficient. Grabbing him, binding him, dragging him out of the yard and after a moment or two of waiting on the street – still no one taking notice of them; passers-by instead lowering their heads, shielding their eyes and hurrying away – they piled with him into the back of a van and drove him away. Grigor Vardanyan guessed that he was going to die. But for which of his crimes and misdemeanours he was going to die he was not yet sure.

Home, for Mickey, was a little terraced house, modest but comfortable and with a bit of a yard out at the back where he could potter and grow vegetables. He had ambitions for an allotment one day, but he rarely spoke of this to anyone else.

As ambitions go, it seemed a modest one, but it presupposed his having time to spend on an allotment and for Mickey *that* ambition – to have time to make things grow – was not only very private, but at times seemed unattainable.

It took him close on an hour to walk back there. Mickey had little patience with public transport and, besides, he liked to walk, using the time to clear his head of the work and get into 'home mode', as Belle liked to call it. It was true that he did discuss his work with his wife. She was a good listener, sensible and concerned, and she also had a fine sense of what should be kept confidential so Mickey never had any worries on that score.

He'd been walking for about ten minutes when the thought occurred to him that he was being followed or, at the very least, that he was being observed. Twice he crossed the road, just to give himself the opportunity to look both ways and back the way he'd come, but the streets were crowded and whoever it was, if it was anyone at all, was clearly being careful.

He paused to look in shop windows, switched his route from the main thoroughfares to the less used back streets as he neared his destination and, once, was certain he caught a flicker of movement as someone dodged out of sight into an entryway.

Mickey backtracked, walking down the centre of the road and looking this way and that, not troubled now that his pursuer might be alerted. He halted at the entry where he was certain he'd seen movement and then ventured a little way down. He could see that it led simply into a shared yard, a water pump and a privy block all there was to see. If there had been a follower, they could have gone in through any of the half dozen doors leading off it, and it was just as likely that Mickey had spotted someone simply heading for home.

He turned slowly and walked back to the street, empty but for a couple of girls playing hopscotch and a group of boys, at the far end, kicking a somewhat deflated bladder against a wall.

Frowning, Mickey continued on home, walking down the middle of the street all the way and pausing at each turn to look back. There was little in the way of traffic in these little roads between terraces. The occasional delivery van and a cart pulled by a piebald horse, carrying a man crying 'anyragbone?' and looking for scrap. Mickey knew him by sight and nodded as he passed, wishing him a fine day.

Almost, Mickey dismissed the thought that he had been observed since parting from Henry. Almost, he decided that he had been mistaken, but Mickey's instincts were good and that small, nagging doubt remained.

He let himself in and called out, 'Belle! I'm back sooner than I expected, love. I thought we might take ourselves out for a spot of lunch.'

Isabella Hitchens came through from the kitchen where she'd been scrubbing and tidying and making herself at home again. Mickey was broad and solid and Belle was small and slight, with a mass of dark hair. She had not given in to the fashion for cropping and shingling, instead wearing it in a coil in the nape of her neck. Mickey caught his breath every time he saw her.

'That sounds like an excellent idea,' she said. She came close and wrapped her arms around him, kissing him with a passion that would have surprised his colleagues. No one really associated Mickey Hitchens with passion. Mickey Hitchens was associated with solidity and a job well done, not with being loved by someone as exotic looking as Belle.

'Good to have you home, lass,' he said. 'Henry sent his best love. Now we have an unexpected afternoon of freedom, let's make the most of it.'

Grigor knew that he would never be free again. He hadn't seen where they had taken him; a sack had been put over his head and pulled tight around his neck. After a while the van had stopped and he'd been hustled out, dragged down some stairs and into a space which echoed loudly. Through that space and into a smaller room beyond, and the door had been closed. When the sack had been removed he had seen Josiah Bailey sitting at a table. Josiah Bailey had a blackjack, loaded with lead shot, in his hand and was tapping it lightly against the table top.

'I've done nothing.' It was the first thing that came into Grigor's head and he realized how pathetic it sounded.

'Everyone's done something, Grigor.' Josiah pointed to a chair and Grigor was pushed down into it, one man pressing on his shoulders and another grabbing his right arm and holding him by the wrist, spreading his hand out flat on the rough, scarred wood of the table.

Grigor screamed, knowing what was to come. Imagining the least of what was to come and fearing the rest, so overcome by fear that he pissed himself.

Josiah Bailey laughed. 'Nothing to worry about at all,' he said, and brought the blackjack down hard on Grigor's hand.

There was no artificial light in the room and the only illumination was through a narrow window high up in the wall. As the afternoon wore on and the light faded, so did Josiah Bailey's interest in the man he had been torturing. Grigor was unconscious now and Bailey had no particular concern about him waking up again. He tossed the blackjack on to the table and signalled to his men to take the body away. He was pondering on what might have been the one useful piece of information gleaned from today's exercise.

'Dalla did it,' Grigor had said. 'It was Dalla. Dalla Beaney.'

NINE

1925

Clement Atkins was pleased with his prize. Ricky Clough seemed less so, with his end of the encounter.

'Clem Atkins. What the 'ell do you want?'

He peered round Clem's shoulder at the man sitting at the bar. An unprepossessing figure in a checked flat cap and black scarf, wound several times around his neck. 'Sabini,' Clough said. 'What's he doing 'ere? You doing business with the Eyeties now?'

'I do business with whoever I like, Cloughie.'

'Does Bailey know that?' Clough grinned at him. 'But I don't suppose he knows anything about this, am I right?'

'In time, Cloughie boy, Bailey will be a distant memory. Now, I've got a bit of a proposition for you, if you might be interested in such a thing.'

Clough crossed to the bar and took the drink from Sabini's hand, sniffed it, then gestured that Sabini should hand him the bottle. 'What sort of proposition?'

'A business proposition.'

'I ain't a fucking businessman. You want someone getting rid of, I'm yer man. That's what I do.' He swallowed the drink, topped up the glass. 'Bailey, is it?' He sounded keen.

'No, not yet. We kill him now, we open us up to trouble. We weaken him first, slide ourselves into place, take over, job done.'

Clough shrugged. 'And how long's that going to take?'

'Long as it does. Sometimes you've got to have a bit of patience to get these things done. But don't worry, Cloughie, you can still keep your hand in. I'm sure we've got a few names you can turn into bodies.'

Clough eyed Clem and then cast a look at Sabini. 'And him?'

'Mr Sabini is a coming man, Ricky. One rises, so does the other.'

Clough shrugged and emptied his glass again. 'So, why bring me back from the dead?' he wanted to know.

'Because Bailey's shit scared of you. And scared is where we want him to be. Weak is what we want him to be. Undermined, so his own people just let him go, and when we move in not a word will be said or a hand lifted.'

Clough shrugged. 'Whatever,' he said. 'It's all the same to me.'

TEN

1928; Sunday

Cynthia's townhouse was lit up like a Christmas tree – though the tree itself would not be installed for another week or so. Henry always tried to be present for tree decoration evening. Cynthia insisted on keeping it as a family affair and she, the children, Henry and usually her husband, Albert, took part in the ritual.

Henry felt she was probably compensating for the lack of celebration when they were both growing up. Apart from a sumptuous Christmas meal – for adults only, and those specially invited guests, certainly not Henry and his sister – there had been little celebration in the Johnstone household. Christmas and birthdays passed largely unacknowledged and one of the things that Cynthia had insisted upon when, at the age of fifteen, she had become responsible for both of them, was that they should 'do Christmas properly'.

'Properly', that first year, had been a tree created of scavenged branches and hawthorn berries threaded on to a long piece of cotton for decoration and a meal cooked on a single burner. Presents of gingerbread and sugar mice – but Henry cherished the memory.

He eased the collar beneath his bow tie and surrendered his coat to the maid. The inside of the house sparkled, illuminated and garlanded, the air heavy with the scent of food and spiced wine. Cynthia had developed a reputation for starting off the Christmas celebrations early and her December parties now marked the start of the festive season for many of her social set. Cynthia had survived and then thrived in the somewhat unforgiving world she had married into by becoming the perfect hostess, though it still rankled that there were certain 'old money' families who would never grant her an entrée.

Taking a glass of champagne that he knew he would

probably not drink, Henry glanced around the room, looking for his sister. His brother-in-law spotted him first and seized his hand.

'Good to see you, old boy. So glad you could make it. We've had a houseful, all damned weekend; hope to scoot the last of them out the door by midnight, what?'

His cheerful tone belied the disparaging words. Henry knew that Albert loved all the attention these gatherings brought. He loved Cynthia and the children too, and in view of this Henry would have been willing to make a great many allowances, but fortunately he quite liked his brother-in-law, even though they had little in common.

'Walter,' – Albert had seized upon a passing guest – 'meet Henry. Cyn's brother, you know, the murder detective.' Albert's grab at his guest's sleeve had unbalanced him and he staggered a few steps sideways before righting himself.

Walter eyed Henry over a glass of champagne. He looked as inebriated as his host. 'Delighted,' he said, extending his hand, and then abruptly withdrew it as his attention was drawn elsewhere. 'I say, isn't that the Mitchum girl?'

'Oh, so it is. Cynthia's through in the blue lounge,' Albert told Henry. 'Catch up later, old bean.'

Henry was much too used to his brother-in-law to take offence and, in truth, rather relieved to have been spared the conversation with Walter – whoever he was – about crime scenes and lurid headlines that inevitably followed such an introduction.

Passing through the main salon, he headed for the blue lounge, a pretty space with walls clad in Chinese wallpaper, furnished with the latest in what Cynthia told him was Art Deco. From the *Exposition Internationale des Arts Décoratifs*, Cynthia had explained. She had attended the exhibition in Paris a few years before, when Albert had been there on business. Cynthia spoke excellent French and passable German – Albert's business interests extended to both countries of late – and so she often went with him on business trips.

Cynthia made sure that she was an asset in all kinds of unexpected ways.

She was standing beside the buffet, in conversation with an

older woman whom Henry did not recognize. Cynthia stood out from the sea of blacks and pastels in a silk dress of emerald green that went well with her dark red hair and pale skin. Her hair was bound with a ribbon that flashed and sparkled as she moved her head and the back of the dress was cut daringly low and held together, so far as Henry could tell, with a tie of the same sparkling fabric, finished with an ornately beaded tassel.

She smiled with pleasure when she saw him. 'Henry! Oh, I am so glad you could make it. Lady Fielding,' she said, turning her attention back to the older woman, 'may I present my brother, Henry Johnstone. Henry, this is Lady Fielding. She's the patron of one of the refugee committees I'm involved with.'

'And you must be the detective.' Lady Fielding shook his hand. 'And now, my dear, I must say my goodbyes. At my age, one reaches nine o'clock and bed begins to call. But call round tomorrow and we'll discuss things further. It's so nice to have a sensible head to converse with.'

She hobbled off, leaning heavily on a black cane topped and tailed in silver.

Cynthia pecked her brother on the cheek. 'So, how the devil are you? It's been weeks.'

Henry smiled. 'It's been two, and we've spoken on the phone four times in between.'

'It's still too long. My God, these people can eat and drink. You'd think they'd been starving themselves for a month, the way they put it all away. You've seen Albert?'

'Briefly. He and someone called Walter, whom I almost met, went off in pursuit of someone called the Mitchum girl.'

'Ah. Walter would be Walter Prendergast, I imagine. He's into coffee and rubber, I believe. The Mitchum girl is Lady Evelyn Mitchum. Just out this year and everyone's falling over themselves to make sure she's married before the season's over. Poor chick, she's never been so popular. I'm hoping she's got the sense not to have her head turned too soon.'

She took Henry's arm. 'So how are you, and how's Mickey? And what dreadful crimes are you investigating this week?'

Henry smiled at his sister. 'Mickey is well and sends his

best regards. As to investigations, you'll no doubt read about it all in tomorrow's papers. It's taken a while for this one to be picked up by the press; the deaths of one known felon and his probable associate, found in the Kentish marshes, don't attract quite so much interest as a victim who seemed more deserving might.'

'Sounds wet and cold,' Cynthia observed.

'Wet and definitely cold. I was grateful for my coat.'

'Which you'd have had a lot sooner if you hadn't been so stubborn. That old one was practically worn through. A sister can give presents to her brother without him fussing, you know.' She patted him on the arm. 'I told Melissa that she could wait up for you. Young Georgie will probably be fast asleep, but she'll be awake and reading. It seems funny not to have Cyril home, but he'll be back soon. School finishes in another week.'

Henry left her and went upstairs to find his niece and nephew. Melissa was ten and George five. Their elder brother, Cyril, had recently become a full-time boarder, a decision Cynthia had been reluctant to make. She had insisted at first that the boys should not go away. Cyril had been a day scholar and then boarded in the week, but since autumn he'd been away full time. His decision; at twelve, he had told his mother that he was old enough to shift for himself and that he was missing out on the fun to be had with his friends at the weekends.

Cynthia had given in. Cyril was a capable boy. Outgoing, sporty and affable, and clearly thriving at school, so she had no real argument.

Melissa had her tutors at home, shared with two other girls, the daughters of Cynthia's friends, and showed no signs of wanting life to change. Young Georgie was already petitioning to go with Cyril, though both Cynthia and Albert were against him being away from home too soon. Albert had boarded from six years old and been thoroughly miserable for the first few years. He had, somewhat surprisingly, dug in his heels and sided with his wife when his father had suggested they were being too soft with the boys.

Henry tapped on the door to the nursery suite and Nanny opened it a crack and peered through.

'You're very late,' she said. 'Five minutes. No more.'

Henry slipped through the playroom, past the rocking horse and doll's house and steam engines, and tapped on Melissa's door. It was already standing half open and he could see his niece propped up against her pillows with a book leaning against her raised knees. She was almost asleep.

Gently, Henry eased the book aside (*Alice in Wonderland* – again) and set it down on her bedside table. She roused a little. 'Hello, Uncle Henry.'

'Hello, Melissa.' He bent and kissed her forehead, stroking the soft brown hair aside. 'You go to sleep now,' he told her. 'I'll arrange with your mother for us both to go out Christmas shopping soon. Would you like that?'

She nodded sleepily and then turned on her side. He watched her for a moment or two as her breathing slowed and settled and she drifted away. He knew he should not have favourites and he did love George and Cyril with an intensity that took him by surprise, but Melissa had a special place in his heart.

Nanny appeared in the doorway and beckoned sternly. 'The young need their sleep,' she said. She yawned and added, 'And so do the old.'

'You aren't old,' Henry told her. 'Nowhere near old.'

He had learned the line from Mickey and discovered that there were certain people even *he* could please by using it. Such social play did not come easily or naturally.

'Get on with you. Now, do you have your diary with you?'

'I do.'

She indicated the calendar hanging above her worktable. 'Well, if you've promised to go shopping, you need to know when Melissa is available. This *is* the party season, you know.'

Henry dutifully noted days when Melissa might be free and then he made his way back down the stairs and wondered if he could legitimately sneak away. After all, he'd done the things he'd come here for.

He paused for a moment, eavesdropping on the conversations in the hall.

His brother-in-law, apparently more sober than Henry had thought, was mid-debate.

'I don't like what I'm seeing over there, that's the long and the short of it. There'll be trouble, you mark my words.'

'Your words or your wife's words?' The tone was jeering and the words distinctly slurred.

'And what do you mean by that?'

'A man should trust . . . trust his own judgement. Women and business . . . like teaching a dog to walk on its hind legs. Funny and all that, but no value to it.'

A burst of laughter drowned out Albert's reply. Henry wondered whether he should go down or stay put. He knew that Albert actually set great store by Cynthia's common sense but that neither of them made great public display of the fact.

He descended a few steps more, picking up the threads of the conversation now that the laughing party had passed on.

'Risk isn't everything,' Albert was saying. 'I've lost enough to know that I like my investments to be safe.'

Henry didn't catch the very slurred response, but he gathered it was insulting. Albert had reddened and now looked positively furious. Henry wandered over and touched his brother-in-law on the arm. 'Just the man,' he said. 'I was hoping for a word before I go.'

Albert glared at him and then looked relieved at the interruption. He excused himself and strode off towards his study. Henry followed him.

'Everything all right?' he asked, closing the door gently behind him. If the blue salon was strictly in the latest style, Albert's study was stuck firmly in the Edwardian era. Leather and wood and deep red walls, a little discoloured now by the inevitable soot from the open fire.

'Yes, yes, it's all fine. I just need a moment to gather my thoughts. Men like that . . .'

'You were discussing Germany?' Henry guessed.

'No, but I might as well have been. You know I gave up on my idea of investing there?'

Henry nodded. 'You dislike the rise of the nationalists,' he said. 'Think it will be bad for business. But not Germany this time?'

Albert sighed. 'No. Truth is, Henry, I've been offered shares in an up-and-coming company, General Securities. Man by the name of Clarence Hatry, reckons he has plans for something he wants to call "United Steel". He seems to think he can pull off some major commodities mergers in the USA and the promise, as always, is for quick profits for investors.'

'And the man you were arguing with?'

'Oh, he's one of Henry Paulet's mob. Paulet is Marquess of Winchester and he's chairman of Hatry's investment company.'

'And you're dubious.'

'Drink?' Albert poured two measures of whiskey without waiting for a response and handed Henry a glass. 'I said I'd think about it, then I had some digging done.' He paused and grinned. 'Cynthia had some digging done. I'm always too ready to jump, old man, and she's always there, ready with the reins. Anyway, it seems this Hatry fella, he's ploughed three major concerns into bankruptcy in the States and each time *he's* come up smelling of roses and left a trail of other poor fellas in the you-know-what. It makes you wonder, doesn't it, what a man like that might do next? So, you see, I'm being Mr Cautious this time. Mr Watch and Wait.'

Henry sipped his drink. 'That sounds sensible to me.'

'Sensible be damned. I'm a dead loss at being sensible. Or I was, until I married your sister and the children came along. These days, I have to admit, I like the quiet life. The risks are tempting but I'm not as keen to suffer the losses. And I don't trust the man.'

Henry wondered whether he meant Hatry or Paulet, or the one he'd been arguing with.

'*And* I've been watching the American markets. You ask me, Henry, they are overstretching, overinvesting – and overstating their expectations. What goes up, Henry, it's going to come down sometime. Like a ton of bricks, and I don't want to be one of those it lands on.'

Henry could hear Cynthia's advice clearly in her husband's words but he was wise enough not to comment on it. Albert seemed eager to change the subject.

'And what about you, old man? Is the policeman's lot still not a happy one?'

'It's been a damned cold one this week,' Henry said with

feeling. 'Two bodies fetched up on the flats just out of a village called Upchurch. And it rained like someone had pulled the plug on some celestial bath tub.'

Albert settled down in one of the wing chairs set beside the fire and gestured to Henry to take the other. 'So,' he said, his earlier fit of pique now forgotten. 'What can you tell me that I won't be reading in the morning papers?'

Henry and Albert were still deep in conversation when the clock struck half past ten and a quiet knock at the door interrupted their flow.

'Probably Cynthia come to tell us we should be mingling,' Albert said resignedly, though he sounded more sanguine about his guests now, ready to rejoin the fray.

Instead, when the door opened, Sergeant Mickey Hitchens stood there, looking apologetic.

'Mickey, my good fellow! Come along in and share some of this rather good whiskey. My dear brother-in-law is failing to keep his end up. He's still on his first glass.'

'Second,' Henry corrected him, though he'd not yet touched it. 'What is it, Mickey?'

'Murder,' Mickey said, shutting the door gently and declining the offer of a drink. 'I've got a car waiting for us outside.'

Albert seemed to sober up in an instant, a trick Henry had witnessed a number of times and still not worked out. 'Go on, Henry. I'll make your apologies to Cynthia. To do with this Kent thing, is it?'

'We don't know yet,' Mickey told him. He turned to Henry. 'They came to fetch me from home. DCI Prothero is already at the scene.'

Henry raised an eyebrow. If Prothero was already there, why did they need him? He followed Mickey across the vestibule and collected his coat. Someone must have pre-warned the maid because she was already at the door, waiting for him.

'What's going on, Mickey?' Henry asked as they hurried down the steps to the waiting car. 'If Prothero is already there . . .'

'Him and the police surgeon,' Mickey said. 'Man called Grigor Vardanyan, we took him in a few years back, if you remember, kiting and receiving.'

Henry nodded. 'Small, ferrety. Armenian, I think?'

'That'll be him. Well, someone beat the life out of him and laid him out on the foreshore, just above the tideline. Constable spotted him on a routine patrol and called it in. Prothero was on the board so he went down. When he saw who it was, he figured we might be interested.'

'He was one of Josiah Bailey's men,' Henry said. 'If I remember, he worked for the father and then the son.'

'And now he's dead, only this time it sounds more like Bailey's style to me. Bailey junior, that is. The father had a bit more subtlety and discretion about him when it came to disposing of the dead.'

We must look a strange sight, Henry thought. They were close to St Paul's and the streets were busy. Onlookers hung over the railings to peer down at them. He himself was still in evening dress, his heavy coat fastened tight and collar turned up over the bow tie. Prothero, as always, the gentleman in appearance. Smartly clad and with a soft voice Henry could never recall having heard raised. His polished shoes were not fit for the mud – neither were Henry's. Only Mickey, fetched from home, had been able to pull on an old pair of oiled leather boots.

The police surgeon, it seemed, had been entertaining dinner guests and Henry was interested to spot a bright red paisley waistcoat beneath his jacket and overcoat.

Constables kept the gathering of onlookers under control as they stared down at the police and at the body. A constable held a blanket to block the view, but the onlookers simply shifted a few feet along and stared down again. The foreshore was a popular spot with mudlarks, Henry knew. Unusual in that a section of shingle beach was left high and dry in all but the spring tides.

He took a step back and surveyed the scene, Prothero coming over to join him.

'Every finger on both his hands is broken. Not just broken, smashed beyond repair.'

'He was known as a card-sharp and for playing three-card Monte. I can't think of a more apt warning. Or punishment. Except this has gone far beyond that.'

Prothero nodded. 'Whatever they wanted to know, he would have told them long before they inflicted the worst of the damage. When they finished with his hands, they smashed his wrists and then worked their way up his arms. It's a vicious act, Henry.'

'When did Grigor last get out of gaol?'

'According to our records, just over a month ago. I hadn't realized he was even back in London.'

Henry nodded. He had described Grigor as a ferret when speaking to Mickey and that was true; he had both the appearance – narrow, sharp and nervy – and the swiftness. Henry would be willing to bet that just about every detective in the central office had arrested or warned off or received information from the dead man at some point or other.

'He was so bent he had to screw his hat on,' Prothero commented. 'But I'd have said he was harmless and relatively blameless as these things go. Never violent and never troublesome in that way.'

'Bailey,' Henry said.

'I'd put money on it. But what the heck did Josiah Bailey want to know so badly?'

Henry sighed. 'You said already that whatever Grigor knew he would have told straight off. Bailey did the rest for sport. Just because he could. When the old man was still around he kept some control over his son. But now . . .'

'Rumour is the father's dead already.'

'I've heard that too, and Bailey's hold on his territories is not what it was. The question is, who is ready to move in and how bad is it going to get as Bailey tries to keep them out?'

'Two – and we have to assume three – of Bailey's associates dead in as many days. What if Bailey didn't do this to Grigor? What if someone is sending a message?'

'I'd rather go with the first option,' Henry said heavily. 'Otherwise we are all in deeper trouble.'

Henry and Mickey accompanied the body back to St Mary's Hospital, the police surgeon having privileges there. They saw him laid out on the mortuary slab and, under better light, made a closer assessment of the injuries.

Gaspard, the police surgeon, would not be carrying out the post-mortem. He had living patients to see in the morning so that task would pass to someone else – St Mary's being one of the major centres for the teaching of forensic science, there would be no shortage of candidates for the job.

'In my view, this was the killing blow,' Gaspard said, turning the head and indicating a deep depression in the back of the skull. 'But I doubt he'd have known much about it by then. The pain would have been considerable. I don't think he'd have been fully conscious by the time the killing blow was administered.'

'I'm thinking a blackjack,' Mickey said, looking at Grigor's hands. 'I've seen injuries similar to this enough times.'

'Then I bow to your superior knowledge,' Gaspard said, unable to keep the distaste from his voice – though whether it was distaste at the injuries or at a non-medical man, a mere police sergeant, claiming better knowledge than himself was something of a moot point.

'Now, if you gentlemen have finished with me, I'd like to get a couple of hours' sleep before I make my rounds in the morning.'

Henry thanked him and Gaspard scurried away.

'I heard what you said to Prothero,' Mickey said. 'You really think we may have the start of a turf war on our hands.'

'As do you,' Henry said. 'As do many of our colleagues. They'd just prefer not to give voice to the possibility.'

'Not talking about something don't make it go away,' Mickey said stoutly. 'How's Cynthia, by the way? And the kiddies?'

'All well. I only saw Melissa. Georgie was asleep and Cyril is away until the end of next week.' They switched out the lights and followed Gaspard up the stairs. The mortuary assistant let them out. 'And what is troubling you?'

Henry, not always the most perceptive of men, was sensitive enough to his sergeant's moods to have noted something more than the tension usual when attending a crime scene.

Mickey nodded. 'When I left you yesterday I chose to walk back home. I had the sense of being followed. Of being observed. I played all the tricks I knew but could catch no one doing either.'

He described to Henry how he thought he had seen a figure dart down an alleyway. 'And now I think of it, I'm sure it was a child.'

'Children are often used as lookouts, as couriers, as tails,' Henry observed. 'No one takes much notice of children in the street. They are as invisible as spies.'

He paused in his steps and looked at Mickey. 'You are bothered by this?'

'I'm bothered by not knowing for certain whether there was anybody, and not knowing for certain what it means if there was. I've told Belle to keep her eyes open, and the neighbours and the local constables too. If there's anyone about that shouldn't be, I'll get to hear of it.'

ELEVEN

While Henry had been at Cynthia's party Bailey's men had been tasked with finding Dalla Beaney and the first place they thought of looking was the encampment in Ash Tree Lane in Gillingham.

A convoy of three vehicles had left the city and driven out in the dark. Parked a distance away and then disgorged their passengers. A dozen of Bailey's hard men, armed and determined and arrogant enough to believe that they could win out against the camp full of gypsies and travellers and fighters.

They came in from three sides, the camp being roughly triangular in shape, and the dogs were barking before they breached the perimeter fence. Men had appeared before they had reached the first vans. They had been in the encampment far less than a minute before they were challenged.

'Who are you and what business have you here?'

The man who spoke had clearly not been disturbed from sleep; he was fully dressed and appeared to be unarmed but was, as one whispered comment had it, 'the size of a brick shithouse'.

Clem hushed him. Bailey had put him in charge and he was not prepared to be intimidated.

The others with the challenger were more wiry but just as determined. Clem stepped forward and in the firelight the gun in his hand could be clearly seen but the big man, though he glanced at it, did not seem intimidated.

'We're looking for Dalla Beaney. Our boss wants a word with her. We've no business with anyone else.'

To Clem's surprise, the big man laughed. 'You tell your boss he'd best get himself one of those spiritualist fellas, then. That's the only way he'll talk to Dalla.'

Clem was surprised enough by the laughter to be shocked into asking what the man meant and his question was greeted with more laughter.

'Are you the best that could be found? Thick as pig shit. I mean the woman is dead, has been this last five years. Tuberculosis and a bad winter took her.'

'And how do we know you're telling the truth?'

There was an almost imperceptible shift in both mood and position among the big man and his companions and, now his eyes were getting used to the dark, Clem could see that others had joined them and that the men who had come with Clem, but entered the camp from the other side, were now held fast. Clem, undaunted, still had his gun and he took several steps forward. 'Gypsies always lie,' he said.

The big man seemed to take no offence. Seemingly still undaunted by the weapon pointed at him, he nodded slowly. 'To outsiders. But not about the dead. No need to lie about the dead. The woman died five years past.'

'And I'm saying I don't believe you.' Clem was convinced that this was a bluff and that the man, though apparently unperturbed, was still a man and would respond, as any man would, to a gunshot. He cocked his revolver and fired one round close to the big man's feet and then all hell broke loose.

Clem and his people found themselves surrounded by men with cudgels and boys with knives and women with cast-iron pans. They had taken up whatever weapons they could grab, and Bailey's men, though they managed to get off the odd shot, found themselves beaten back. Clem was grabbed, the big man's arms wrapped from behind around his chest. His weapon fell to the ground and he felt himself choking and breathless, his ribs cracking under the strain. Finally he was dropped to the ground and kicked, in the buttocks and the ribs and the head, and when he felt sure that he could no longer breathe, he was hauled back to his feet and given a shove that sent him staggering back towards the perimeter fence. Through a haze he heard a shotgun discharge and then a second, but when he attempted to look back he was met with further blows and shoves. He raised his arms to protect his face and then turned away, fled back to the safety of the waiting cars.

Bloodied and bleeding, what was left of Bailey's contingent made it back to their vehicles. Three were missing and Clem was told that two for certain were dead. They didn't know about the third, a young man by the name of Bates who had only recently joined Bailey's crew. This was meant to have been his chance to prove himself.

'I saw him go down,' Clem was told. 'Three of them beating on him with cudgels.'

Clem gave the order to return to base; he was in half a mind to turn tail and run, and only the presence of others in the car stopped him. 'But we had guns,' he said, pre-empting what he knew Bailey would say. 'We had fucking guns and we were bested by a rabble of gypsies.'

He looked at his watch. The whole episode had taken less than half an hour.

Back at the camp they were taking account of their own wounded. No deaths, thankfully. But a few cracked heads that would take some dealing with and two bullet wounds that would need some explaining when the police arrived, as they surely would. Close neighbours to the camp would have heard the rampage and the gunfire and would have reported it.

The big man, Fred, was used to dealing with such concerns and within minutes he had everyone organized. No one took notice of a flatbed leaving in the middle of the night and their own wounded were patched up and put to bed. The children knew better than to speak to the police and Fred handed over the role of liaison to Sarah, sister to the late Dalla Beaney and a woman of status within their community.

The camp was quiet when the police arrived an hour later, a sergeant and two constables, cycling into camp and propping their bikes by the gate. A camp fire was burning close by and a man rose to greet them.

'We heard reports of a disturbance.'

The man shrugged. 'Two of our young 'uns out late, drunk more than they should have done, got into an altercation over some card game or other. A few of the local lads followed them back in and they set to brawling. Our Sarah sorted them, mended heads and sent the rest on their way.'

'Then we'd like a word with *our Sarah*,' the sergeant told him.

The man shrugged and directed him towards Sarah's caravan. Now the children were old enough to set up on their own she had her own vardo, and lived with just her husband. She opened the door and came out to them, wrapped in a large shawl.

She and the sergeant had had dealings on several occasions and he knew he would get nothing out of her that she didn't want to say, and she knew that he would go away satisfied with her explanation because it was too much trouble for him to do otherwise. She repeated the story that the sergeant had already heard.

'Our Billy got a black eye and his head cracked,' she said. 'So I've bedded him down here for the night.'

'I'll need to see him.'

'You'll not set foot inside. This is my home. You may look through the door.'

The sergeant nodded and she opened the door a little wider. Her son Billy lay on one of the bunks. He roused himself briefly and looked the sergeant in the eyes.

'Got into a fight, did you?'

'A bit of one.'

The sergeant stood for a moment, considering. He knew there was more to it than he was being told. And he also knew that he wasn't going to get any further or any deeper into the matter. He and Sarah had their script and so far they were sticking to it.

'I'm told there was gunfire.'

Sarah shrugged. 'One of the men might have fired into the air. The little bastards didn't want to break it up and go on their way.'

'Language,' he said, mildly.

'I'd defy you to be polite if a rabble came and disturbed your night. We deal with our own; go and deal with the idiots who followed ours back. They should think theirselves lucky they got off with a few bruises.'

'And it's no good my asking who these others were.'

'No good asking me, and I don't suppose Billy knows names. Just kids, the lot of them, and stupid with it.'

'I'll have the constables come back in the morning, look around.' The last piece of the script.

Sarah closed the door to her van. 'Best keep the heat in,' she said.

She watched as the sergeant and his constables left and then retreated into the vardo.

Once the police had gone, Fred knocked on her door. She came out on to the steps again to speak to him. 'Why would they come looking for my sister?'

'Only one reason I can think of. The same reason that brought her back here in the first place.'

Sarah nodded. She couldn't think of any alternative either.

'You best give the young 'uns a warning. If Bailey sent his thugs here then the chances are they'll be looking for them too.'

'I'll go to the telephone at first light, see if I can catch Malina before she goes off to work. My sister is dead and gone, they should be leaving her bones to rest in peace.'

Fred paused. 'It never seemed to me that she had much peace living,' he said after a while. 'Not even after she came back here. If you know what was bothering her, Sarah, then you best try and put it right. Or they'll be back again and they'll be more prepared this time.'

'I'll give it thought,' she said. 'But my sister was as close mouthed as our ma was. I know she was hiding something, but she never told me what. I know whatever it was, it weighed on her conscience, but she wouldn't speak it, not even when she knew she was dying. She didn't want to taint the kids.

'And she never made confession. At least not so far as I know. She went to her death with whatever it was on her conscience, so she'll not rest easy until it is put right. And neither will her young, no matter how much she tried to protect them. Better for them to know, so we can lay that to rest too.'

TWELVE

Mickey had reached home just after four a.m. Belle was up, waiting for him, wrapped in a blanket in front of the fire.

'I thought you might be cold,' she said. 'So I kept the fire going. The kettle's hot. Would you like some tea?'

Mickey watched contentedly as she warmed the pot and then poured boiling water on to the leaves and set it by the hearth.

'Bad, was it? I'm guessing it was if Prothero called you and Henry out there.'

'A man called Grigor Vardanyan. You may have run across him. He was from your neck of the woods.'

She frowned for a moment. 'Small man, had a three-card Monte pitch? Bailey used him as an informant, if I remember right. He was good at watching and listening.'

'That'll be the one. He either watched the wrong thing, listened to the wrong thing or failed to report those things back to Bailey. We don't know yet, but what Bailey did to him was vindictive and cruel.'

'And why should that surprise you?' Belle had grown up a few streets from Bailey's family. She had moved away at fourteen and had been making her own way ever since. Her parents had left London only a short time afterwards. She and Mickey had met ten years earlier, when she had been only eighteen, and had met again some time after that and been married within a month. It was perhaps the only impulsive act that Mickey could ever have been accused of, and they had been married now for just short of five years. At twenty-eight, Belle was almost eleven years younger than her husband.

'So, you'll be off again in the morning, then?'

'Got to grab a few hours' sleep, then the boss wants to go back to Rainham. He thinks we need to look at Otterham Creek again. Get some more local knowledge on this.'

'So how does he think it's all connected up?'

'I think he's got about as much idea as I have at the moment. But we're just as concerned that it *isn't* Bailey as we are that it is. If someone is trying to move in on his territory it could escalate fast, and none of us want that.'

Belle nodded. 'Best go to bed, then,' she said. 'I had a chat to the neighbours about strangers hereabouts, maybe a child. Mr Briggs, three doors down, he thinks he might have seen something, or rather someone. A skinny little kid, about ten or twelve, not local. Briggs must've been walking down just after you came home and he spotted the child looking at door numbers. He thought he might be looking for someone and asked if he could help, but the boy just ran off. Might be nothing, of course.'

'I'll have a chat with Mr Briggs before I go in tomorrow. Like he says, it might be nothing. I might have been imagining things.'

Belle smiled at him. 'For that, you'd have to have an imagination,' she said.

THIRTEEN

At seven o'clock the following morning Sarah phoned the residential club in Guilford Street where her niece was staying. She had a room there, with a little stove and shared bathroom. Ten other girls roomed on the same floor and she had friends amongst them. A caretaker and his wife minded the place and there was a phone in the vestibule where residents could call out and friends and relatives could call in. The concierge or his wife would then go and fetch them to the phone. Sarah had only done it twice before; she rarely used the phone and was hoping she had enough change for the call box and that her niece hadn't left for work already.

It turned out that she just caught her: Malina was on her way downstairs when the caretaker's wife came to find her.

Quickly, Sarah filled her in about the night's events.

'But why would anyone come looking for Ma?'

'That we don't know. We don't know whose men they were, though we can make a few guesses.'

'You mean Josiah Bailey? Isn't he dead?'

'The old man might be, but not the son. From what I hear, the son is far worse than his father ever was. You just keep looking over your shoulder, girl, and try and get word to Kem, if you can. Now this Bailey knows your ma's dead, he might come looking for you.'

'But we don't know anything.'

'Since when has knowing anything mattered to anyone?' Sarah said.

Malina was very thoughtful as she made her way to work. She'd started off in the typing pool and worked her way up so that she was now one of the secretaries shared by a commercial office that dealt with imports and exports, ten minutes' walk away from her lodgings. She didn't particularly like the work, but it was a job and the pay wasn't bad for a girl her age. This phone call from Sarah bothered her a great deal. She remembered the night they fled their cottage – or rather had been forced to flee. Remembered it clear as day, and remembered the effort she had put in afterwards, trying to get her mother to tell her what had caused the problem and who had killed their father.

And why.

By seven a.m. Josiah Bailey had already spent several hours venting his anger on the returning men, and most of all he blamed Clem. Blamed him all the more because he wasn't present to take the blame. As they'd come back through Gillingham, Clem had made a decision. He'd stopped the car and waited for the others to pull up behind him. Clem Atkins was a single man with no family to suffer retribution for his actions, and the mood his boss had been in these past weeks, he didn't give much for his own chances.

He was quite blunt about it. 'I'll not be going back with you. Any of you that are of the same mind, we'll take one of the cars and we'll disappear. The rest of you can tell whatever story you like. Tell him we died in the gypsy camp. If you want, tell him you don't know what became of us. He'll hold me to blame, none of you will suffer for it.'

Clem paused and looked from one face to the next. The eight men left to him of the twelve who had gone out that night. He could see their uncertainty, and their fear. Five of them he knew were family men and tied quite closely to Bailey because of that. They would not leave their families to suffer. The others were single, young, their path not yet set, and these three shuffled uncertainly and looked to him for guidance.

'Not easy to disappear with no cash, no nothing,' one finally said.

'But not impossible.' Clem paused. 'I can give each of you a bit of walking round money; once we get away from here we can figure something out. But I've had it. I go back and I'm a dead man.'

'Run and you're a dead man. He won't stop looking for you.'

Clem shrugged. 'I'm all for taking a chance,' he said.

'Besides, I reckon he's got enough on his plate at the moment without chasing after me. I'm small fry. Disposable.'

There had been arguments, but Clem had finally got his way and he and two of the others took a car and left the rest of the group behind. He had no idea whether he was doing the right thing, only that *some* chance is better than no chance – and no chance was what he figured he had if he went back and reported what had happened that night.

Bailey's anger had been hot at first. At first he hadn't believed the story. Couldn't believe that twelve armed men had been defeated by a rabble of largely unarmed gypsies. They all had the sense not to say that some of the fighters had been women; that would have been the final straw. Even if Bailey had spared the rod they'd never have lived it down. And Bailey was in no mood to spare the rod. He took out his anger on two of the older and most experienced men of the group, forcing the others to hold them while he punched and kicked and bent and broke, and then left them half alive on the floor.

His anger turned cold then, his changing mood taking everyone by surprise as he straightened up and wiped the blood from his hands.

'No more,' he said. 'No more foolishness, no more failures. The line is drawn now. And they are going to pay.'

He'd been gone for several minutes before anyone dared to ask who *they* were. Those encamped at Ash Tree Lane? There was something in his tone that suggested larger issues and his comments chimed with what Clem had said about the man having enough on his plate.

'He's not been right since Cloughy came back,' someone muttered. He was hushed immediately.

'If he'd been with us last night, it would have gone off a bit different. You bet your sweet life on it.'

'You want to share space with that mad bugger?'

No one made comment after that. The trouble was, Bailey didn't just own them; he owned a community, and a community couldn't do what Clem had done and just flit when the going got too much.

They helped the injured men home, those that had held

them fast while Bailey took his pleasure with fists and feet and blackjack. One had a knee that would never mend, another was now missing an eye and had a head wound that bled ferociously. They helped them home, and helped wives get the wounded into bed, and no one so much as said a word about what had happened to them. And no one, weeping and grieving and scared though they might be, no one was stupid enough to ask.

The post-mortem took place at St Mary's; it had been squeezed into the schedule early, but it told Henry and Mickey little they had not already surmised.

Grigor had been beaten slowly and systematically, probably over a number of hours and probably with the same weapon. It was only the death blow that was different and the fragments of plaster and whitewash suggested that he had been shoved backwards and his head smashed into a wall.

Henry and Mickey left St Mary's and began their journey back to Upchurch. This time they had a car at their disposal and Mickey drove. Both men were tired and somewhat dispirited and the weather seemed to reflect their mood. A cold slush of snow and rain fell steadily and the windscreen wiper struggled to clear it away.

'So, Grigor Vardanyan.' Henry was looking through the file he had brought along. 'A varied career. Arrived in England in 1912, in the company of his parents and a younger sibling who died of Spanish flu in 1918. He was nine years old when he arrived in this country and only twenty-five when he died. Recently released, after an eighteen-month sentence for fraud.'

'What kind of fraud?'

'Nothing sophisticated. Stole a cheque book, cashed two of the cheques, but unfortunately for him the bank cashier knew the owner of the account by sight and Grigor was clearly not a sixty-year-old man with a grey beard.'

'Belle says he had a three-card Monte pitch since he was a little kid. Says he was a runner for Bailey senior, and the present Josiah Bailey used him as a casual informant. A man like that hears things, sees things, is sensitive to the mood on the streets, I suppose.'

Henry nodded. 'The very reasons *we* might use one of his ilk as an informant. So, he was younger than Billy Crane and Max Peterson, but almost certainly known to them. And involved in petty crime from a very young age.' He paused. 'Not that this in itself is a signifier of anything. Many children steal or practise deceit of one sort or another just to survive, and it's a long stretch from standing on a street corner and duping a crowd playing Find the Lady, to whatever it was that brought such violence down on his head. He'd have paid his dues to Bailey's family, even as a boy.'

'Speaking of children, just after I'd arrived home a boy was spotted in our street, looking at the door numbers. A neighbour asked if he was looking for someone in particular and apparently he took to his heels.'

'Description?'

'Ten or twelve, skinny and underfed . . . nothing that might be useful. But it's a common enough diversion: use a child to scout an area before his elders move in upon a victim or a house to be broken. A child can be of use, posted through a window.'

'True, but as a method of operation it's more commonly used in those parts of town where something would be gained from breaking a house. No offence, Mickey, but if anyone on your street has aught worth the effort, I'd be surprised.'

'There's always the rent money or the gas meter,' Mickey reminded him.

'True . . . but the child was poor enough at the task to be spotted – twice. Once by you and once by a neighbour. I'm reminded of our sailorman and his boy.'

'It crossed my mind,' Mickey agreed, 'but how would the lad have found his way to me?'

'I agree, it would be a stretch.' He fell silent then, allowing the different threads of the case to unravel in his mind.

Mickey, used to his silences, peered ahead through the thickening rain and sleety snow and let him be.

Sergeant Frith had returned to the camp at Ash Tree Lane that morning and he and his constables had made a cursory search of the area, questioned Sarah again and generally made a nuisance of themselves as the daily life of the camp went on around them. Kids and dogs running here and there, horses tethered where they could graze. Some cooking in the camp still happened communally, over the fires dotted about the site. Others used the small stoves in the caravans. On such a cold and bitter day the heat of the fires was welcome and Sergeant Frith paused for a moment to warm his hands.

'You finished here?' Sarah asked him.

'I may have done. Then again, maybe I've not.' He studied her closely. About forty years old, he guessed, her hair starting to grey, but she had fine strong features and intense, intelligent dark eyes that always surprised him. Frith dismissed most of the 'gypsy rabble', as he thought of them, as little more than worthless but on occasion he was forced to make a reassessment. This woman carried herself with such pride, such authority, he was never sure whether he wanted to admire her for it or beat it out of her. Frith did not like to feel such confusion.

The community at the camp, if you could call it a community – Frith was reluctant to do that, it sounded too civilized – consisted mostly of agricultural workers. A few still dealt in horses, but they were off travelling most of the year and only returned in the dead of winter, so that now there were few horses on the field. At this time of year, too, there were a few showman's vans present; those with travelling fairs and circuses sometimes used this as a stopping point. It was more normal for that type, Frith thought, to show up after Christmas, when they rested up for a month or two before the spring season started.

They'd done some house-to-house enquiries that morning and there were several reports of noise from the night before, but one was particularly interesting.

'I heard it was more than a bit of a brawl last night,' he said now.

'And what idiot told you that?' She was watching him as carefully as he was observing her. An uneasy truce existed between them. Frith was more decent than most of the officers she had encountered, but she wouldn't have trusted him as far as she could spit (though she was far too well mannered to spit).

'A witness tells me that there were three cars travelling in convoy. They parked a few hundred yards up the road. Around a dozen men, split up into three groups, got out of those cars, and what is more, they were carrying weapons. Guns.'

She shrugged. 'Well, they didn't come here.'

'And we both know you wouldn't tell me if they did. My witness tells me that these men prowled around your perimeter fence and hedge and seemed prepared to force their way through. My witness could not see all of them, of course; he doesn't have superhuman vision. Then there was a lot of noise and some shooting. A great deal of shouting and screaming, which went on for perhaps ten or fifteen minutes, and then a group of men broke cover and ran back to their cars. They took off like they had the hounds of hell after them, according to my witness.'

This last part was an exaggeration. The witness had simply said that they had driven off at speed.

'You can imagine how intrigued my witness was by all of this, and doubly intrigued to see a truck, one of yours, drive out only a few minutes after that. A funny time to be doing business, Sarah.'

'Some people like to travel by night,' she said. 'Get a head start on the day. It ain't no crime.'

The two constables had finished their prowl and now came back to the fire. The sergeant could see from their faces that they had nothing much to report. No one had let them into their vans or their tents or their cabins. And though Frith could have forced the matter and bashed down a few doors, he knew there was nothing to be gained by that. Whatever was going on here, he would have to discover it by another route.

'You'll be going now, then?'

'We'll be going,' Frith agreed, 'but we'll be back. You know that. From the sound of all of this there's trouble, and there may be more trouble brewing, and I'm not having that on my patch. I'll give you your due, you lot mostly behave yourselves, but you step out of line and I'm warning you, the whole weight of the law will come down on you.'

She tilted her head on one side and gave him a look that

she might have given a child who was telling tall stories. 'You reckon?' she said.

He watched her as she walked away. Arrogant bitch, he thought. What did she have to be so proud about?

FOURTEEN

At mid-morning Malina was sent out on an errand and returning, she passed the local newsagent. Outside on the A-frame was a headline: 'Three Men Dead in Gang Violence'.

Sarah's news fresh in her mind, she took the chance to slip inside the newsagent and buy copies of two of the daily papers, folding them small enough to slip inside her bag so that her purchases would not be noticed and she would not be accused of loitering. It was not until midday, and her legitimate lunch break, that she had time to look past the headlines. The name Max Peterson she did not know but she recognized Billy Crane, both by his name and from the photo – a police mug shot – at the side of the article.

Malina felt her heart begin to race. Billy Crane had changed little since the night he'd come to the cottage and broken their lives apart. She had hated him for it ever since.

There was a third man featured in a different story and this man Malina recognized and had once known well. He had been just a little older than Malina and Kem but they had played with him, and she remembered him most for his unusual sleight of hand. 'Grigor,' Malina whispered. 'What have they done to you?'

In growing dismay she read the reports and the speculation about his injuries – that he'd been tortured before he died. She had liked him; he'd made her laugh. Not the brightest button in the box, maybe, but he'd been kind and that counted for a lot as far as Malina was concerned.

She wondered if Kem had seen the newspapers and how she could reach him. She had no idea where the sailing barge he crewed might be.

Lunch over, she returned to her work somewhat distracted, forcing herself to concentrate on the shorthand as she took dictation, a little piece of her mind worrying at the problem all afternoon.

Having dropped the luggage at the Crown at Upchurch, Henry and Mickey and the local constable they had met previously went back to where they had found the bodies. They drove as far as they dared and then walked the rest of the distance. The rain had stopped, but Henry could tell it was only a pause.

They stood looking across the brown winter reeds at Otterham Creek.

'Tell me about this place,' Henry said. 'Who uses this waterway, what for, how busy might it get? What would bring a boat down here?'

'Across this side, not a lot. The creek gets shallow, and the mud is unpredictable. You can see those jetties there, and there.' The constable pointed with his right hand to two slender lines hugging the bank. 'One of those is for the brickworks and the other for offloading in a more general sort of way. Either way you need to wait for the tide to be high and you need a boat with a shallow draft, like a sailing barge or a lighter.'

'A lighter?'

'A steel hull with a flat bottom. They are rowed by lightermen, though you won't find any such out here. They work in the docks, moving cargo between vessels.'

'Lightermen I have heard of,' Henry said.

'In that direction' – he pointed with his left hand this time – 'is Otterham Wharf. You can't quite see it from this direction because there's a curve, but there'll be boats moored there. And there are buoys just offshore that the boats tie up to, usually when they're waiting for the tide or the wind to change. Once you get out to the mouth of the creek, things get busy. You're not far from the mouth of the Thames and the Medway, where the two rivers meet.

'You've got to know the shoals and the mud flats and the reaches.' He paused, then explained, 'All of these narrow little creeks leading out, they can be unpredictable and dangerous if you don't know the area. There are wrecks and there are shoals and there are shallows. It is not a kind land and it is not kind water. You must be hardy to make a living here, wet or dry.'

'But what interest would there be for a man like Bailey? Is this a place known for smuggling?'

'It's been known.' The constable nodded. 'You show me a bit of water where it hasn't. But this is not a place where there's been much in the way of trouble, not for many years.'

'Not for many years?'

'During the war we had a few arrests of so-called spies. There was that photographer up at Sheerness who was deported in the August of 1914. Lived in Sheerness forty years he had, but you never know, do you? And then an artist chap, got spotted drawing where he shouldn't. That was on Sheppey. I don't know what happened about him, but if you ask me it was more noise and thunder than reality.'

Henry nodded. If you took the Defence of the Realm Act to the letter, it could be read as technically illegal even to have pen and paper in a public place.

'Then there was a farmer, out past Cooper's place, killed his daughter because she got pregnant with the wrong man. That was a nasty business, but it was pure domestic, nothing criminal, apart from the killing.'

'I'd like to look back through your records. Because we know the background, we might notice something that you would not realize was important,' Henry said.

'You're welcome to look them over. I keep a good report of everything.' The constable sounded slightly offended at Henry's tone and Mickey was quick to say, 'I'm sure you do, but you may only have part of the information.'

'You can think of nothing more? It does not have to be recent,' Henry said.

'It would help if I knew what you were looking for, what sort of event you might be thinking about,' the constable said.

It would indeed, Henry thought. He felt as though he were feeling his way through thick fog. He knew that there should be firm ground beneath his feet, but was conscious that it could fall away at any moment and he could end up in mire and bog and deep water.

'We should be heading back,' Mickey said. 'We are about to get very wet.'

FIFTEEN

It was just before four o'clock that afternoon when the captain of the *Lady Bay* went ashore to get their orders. They were tied up at North Woolwich and Kem was fidgety and ready for the off.

At half past four, the captain returned and told him that they were to sail to Millwall to pick up a load from a ship just docked there, but looking at the tides he saw that they would not be able to enter the dock until about one in the morning and so there was no sense setting off yet. The captain had friends berthed up and went for a last visit before they left and Kem, second hand on the boat, made himself some tea and then settled in his cabin in the fo'c'sle to skim through the newspapers the skipper had brought on board.

For some time he sat in his bunk, mug of tea growing cold in his hand as he stared at the headlines, the same articles that his sister had read earlier that day. Billy Crane was dead, Max Peterson too, and so was Grigor. Unlike his sister, he knew Peterson by sight, having seen him once or twice in company with Billy Crane.

Working on the docks, Kem had more contact with the streets and people he'd known as a small child, and still saw a few of their mother's old neighbours.

Kem felt the colour drain from his face as he read the reports for the second time, scouring for detail that he might have missed. What was going on here? He looked for some reference to Tommy Boswell, but there seemed to be none, and Kem wasn't sure what to make of that. By rights Tommy should be gone as well, and Grigor should be living.

The captain returned and they turned in to try and grab a few hours' sleep, knowing that the following day, from midnight on, would give them little time to rest. Kem could not settle. He thought about asking permission to go ashore, to find a phone box and call his sister, but that would lead to all sorts of questions that he didn't want to answer just now. Nothing for it, he would have to wait.

A little before midnight he went up on deck and lit the port, starboard and stern lamps and they eased out from their berth, pushing off from the buoy between close-packed barges and lighters. Once clear they set sail, tacking slowly down the river, reducing sail once the docks were in sight and then waiting in line outside the dockyard gates for the tide to turn.

A little after one a.m. the lock gates opened and the loaded barges were towed out by a tug and then let free to trim sail and take off downriver. The *Lady Bay* waited her turn to be towed into the dock and the lock gates once again closed. The water was brought up to the level of the water in the dock and then the inner gates were opened and the barges towed through. All this time of waiting and slow movement and waiting some more chafed Kem in a way that it did not usually. He was used to the routine and the literal ebb and flow in both tide and work. But he was restless today, unable to think straight, unable to get the pictures of the dead out of his mind.

His thoughts were briefly interrupted as they prepared to pull into their berth. There was the usual tugging and heaving of rope and line and boat hook before they were tied up beside the cargo ship and waiting to be loaded. Knowing that nothing would happen that night the skipper told Kem to turn in for a while. They made tea and he took it back to his bunk, knowing that he wouldn't sleep. He wanted to talk to Malina; she must have seen these reports and be as worried as he was. The past always comes back to bite you, that's what she'd always told him, and now he was certain she was right.

Kem must have managed to doze because when the alarm went at six it found him sleeping. He made more tea and then checked the decks one more time for anything that would impede the loading, before he and the captain opened the hatches. It was then a matter of keeping out of the way as the stevedores brought their sacks across the Jacob's ladder and into the hold.

Kem went below and cleared away their breakfast things. He brought the newspapers back into the galley and was looking through them again when the captain came down. The captain sat and glanced through the newspapers and Kem found that he wanted to talk, but didn't dare. What would he say? In the end he said, pointing to the article about Grigor, 'We knew him, me sister and me, he were just a bit older than us growing up.'

His captain glanced up, one eyebrow raised. 'Sorry to hear that, lad. Close friends, were you?'

Kem considered for a moment and then shook his head. 'No, not close. But it's still a shock. See someone you know in the papers and they're dead.'

The captain nodded sympathetically and then returned to his reading and Kem turned back to his tasks, getting the food on the stove that they would eat at lunchtime.

A little later he wandered back up on deck to watch the loading until twelve noon sharp, when everyone broke for lunch. The stevedores returned to shore and he went back below. It was only when they were berthed up that he and the captain ate together, but his captain was not much for conversation and Kem often read a book. Today was no exception. But he found he couldn't concentrate on the words. They seemed to dance around on the page and his gaze kept straying back to the newspapers. He hadn't quite told the truth, he now realized. There had been a time when he and Malina and Grigor had been very good friends. A time when Grigor had been soft on Malina – not that she was having any of it. A lot of the boys had been soft on Malina, if Kem were honest. She was a good-looking girl, and nice with it. And, if she'd had a mind, she could have been married with children of her own by now.

Kem figured that they'd both been put off that because of their mother's choices and their father's behaviour.

Though he would like to find a girl, Kem thought. Someone to settle with. A bit of peace. That would be nice.

At one o'clock the stevedores returned and the loading was completed in another couple of hours. The captain checked the tally on his list and, seeming satisfied, told Kem that it was time to pull away. Other barges were waiting to be loaded as they eased back away from the ship and into a quiet berth where they could clean the decks down. Kem swept and tidied and they replaced the hatches and tarpaulins and battened everything down. The captain got their papers signed, clearing them to leave the dock, and they made their way further downriver to berth up for the evening and wait for their turn to go back through the lock gates when the tides were right.

It was evening before Kem got his opportunity to go ashore. He stocked up with provisions for the journey and then found a phone box and called his sister. He waited, impatient and frustrated, while she was fetched to the phone and there was no preamble in his conversation.

'Have you seen the papers?'

'Yes, I've seen. And Sarah phoned. Reckons some men were sent to the camp, looking for our mam. Didn't know she was dead. Sarah says we're to watch our backs.'

'Damned right. Malina, what do we do?'

'We hold our nerve, that's what. Look, Kem, you'll be at sea, there's nothing you can do and there's nothing they can do to you while you're out there. No one knows how to find you, no one knows you got a connection to all of this, so just calm down and hold your nerve.'

'And what about you?'

'I'll be careful, that's what about me.'

He had few coins left and could not keep feeding the phone box. 'Let's meet on Sunday, like we said.'

'Of course we will. I love you, little brother.'

'I love you too. You be careful, won't you?'

'I'm always careful,' she told him.

Ken made his way slowly back to the barge and stowed the provisions. It was just on nine in the evening and they would be slipping their moorings in a few hours and joining the other boats in the lock basin, ready to be released back into the river.

The captain came below and checked the provisions as he always did, more out of habit than because he didn't trust Kem to do a good job. 'You call that sister of yours?'

Kem was surprised. 'Yes, I managed to get hold of her.'

'I expect she was shocked too.'

'She was, yes.'

The skipper sat down and filled his pipe, tamping the tobacco gently and checking the draw before lighting it. Kem waited to see if he was going to say any more, but it seemed that the conversation was over and Kem made his way back to his own bunk for a couple of hours of peace, if not sleep, before the voyage began.

That evening Henry and Mickey had a visit from a Sergeant Frith. He had an interesting story to tell about an incident at a gypsy encampment the night before. He had come to them, he said, via a rather roundabout route. A local situation such as a brawl at Ash Tree Lane would not normally have been of interest to Scotland Yard, but on this occasion some strange information had come to light.

He settled with his pint in the bar at the Crown and took a gulp of beer before he started on his tale.

'We've been on alert, you see, because of those two bodies being found and possible links to London criminal activity. I understand, sir, that you and your sergeant have been down here before on this business.'

Henry acknowledged that they had.

'Well, we was called out to the gypsy camp last night, or rather in the early hours this morning, and we were spun this tale about there being a brawl between town lads and gypsy lads which had spilled over into the camp after a drinking session. All very possible, of course, but,' – he paused to tap the side of his nose – 'as I'm sure you'll agree, sir, you get a nose for this kind of thing. Especially among their sort. Gypsies always lie, so they say, and this lot certainly aren't concerned about telling the likes of me the truth.'

'And what do you think happened?' Mickey asked him. He could see by something in Henry's manner and the stiffness of his pose that Henry had taken an instant dislike to this man and therefore it had better be Mickey who asked the questions.

'Well. There, you see. I knew there was something but I didn't quite know what it might be and then we did some enquiring the following morning and we turned up a witness to some strange goings-on. Three cars, they said, driving in convoy to about a hundred or so yards away from the gypsy camp. Twelve men got out, armed with weapons. Guns, you see. Then, they said, all hell broke loose and there was noise and gunfire and these men came hurtling out as though the devil was behind them, got in their cars and drove away.'

Mickey glanced at Henry, but he was concentrating on his whiskey glass and paying very little attention – or so it seemed.

'And did they say much about these men? Their appearance, what weaponry they were using? Did they take the registration numbers of the cars?'

'Well, no. I don't imagine they thought about any of those things.' The sergeant looked awkward all of a sudden. 'Thing is, you see, my witness was just a young lad. Thirteen years old, couldn't sleep and were sitting by his window, reading a book by the street lamp outside. He didn't dare put his own light on because his mother would have told him he should have been in bed, but he confessed things to her in the morning and when she saw us out and about, she came out and fetched me in and the boy told me. I believe he's telling the truth. I know it frightened him.'

'And have you spoken about this witness to anyone?' Mickey asked.

Frith looked even more uncomfortable. 'When we went back this morning, I took my constables and we searched the place and yes, I did mention that there might be a witness to what went on. I was hoping I might shock someone into saying something that they shouldn't. Fat chance of that, with Sarah Cooper,' he added in a moment of honesty.

'Cooper?' Henry questioned. It was an odd coincidence that the cart had been borrowed from Cooper's farm. He wrote Sarah Cooper's name in his notebook and put a question mark beside it.

'You didn't think that you might be putting your witness at risk?' Mickey asked.

'No,' the sergeant said stoutly. 'I'm sure I did not.'

'Who is this boy?' Henry asked.

Frith had the address already written down and he slid it across the table towards Henry. Mickey picked it up. 'And how close is the house to the gypsy camp?'

'A couple of hundred yards away. The cars parked up close by, that's how he managed to see the guns, I suppose.'

'And he was certain that shots were fired?'

Sergeant Frith nodded. 'He was sure about the shotgun fire because he had heard that before. They sometimes go off after rabbits, the local farmer is glad to get rid of the vermin. But he said he heard other bangs, too, that sounded different.'

'Warn the mother we'll be calling on them tomorrow morning,' Henry said. 'I thank you for the information. If it's accurate, it may be useful to us.'

Sergeant Frith realized he'd been dismissed and he downed the rest of his pint and left with great rapidity.

'Interesting,' Mickey said. 'We just have to hope that if this is true, Frith has not endangered a witness.'

'I doubt the encampment will want to make problems with their neighbours, and it could be nothing, just an excitable child who's seen something he does not understand, and whose imagination has filled in the rest.'

'True,' Mickey agreed, 'but in my experience, boys of thirteen or fourteen who are interested in cars and weaponry are usually quite astute in recognizing them. He was disturbed enough to confess to his mother in the morning that he'd not been in his bed.'

Henry conceded the point. 'If we are assuming that these are Bailey's men, what interest do they have in a gypsy camp? This gets more complex. And if word gets out that the boy has seen these men, and could perhaps identify them . . . That might be where the trouble will lie. We will speak to the boy and his mother in the morning and also visit this gypsy camp. I think it's important that we get the lie of the land that way. There are presently too many threads, Mickey, and none of them seem to tie together, at least not in any satisfactory manner. It's interesting that he mentioned a Sarah Cooper. The second time that surname has cropped up. I wonder if there might be a connection.'

'It's not an uncommon name,' Mickey said. 'But yes, it may be meaningful.'

Constable Hargreaves arrived just as the landlord had told them that supper was ready. He brought two large logbooks and a stack of folders in a cardboard grocery box. They invited the constable to remain, suspecting that it might be useful to have him explain his own notes, and Mickey tucked them under the table while they ate. It was to be hoped that there would be something there that would help them understand the connections between Billy Crane and Grigor and an encampment of gypsies and Josiah Bailey.

After supper they retired to a corner of the snug, out of the way of the regular customers, and settled themselves to business. Constable Hargreaves was past the age when he might have retired, but replacements willing to take on the burden of such a large patch were not easy to find. And besides, it was usually quiet, local disputes that could be sorted with a word in the right ear and a reprimand in another. It did mean that he had a long memory of the place; Henry hoped that that would be useful to them now.

The steak and kidney pie for supper had been well prepared and Mickey declared himself 'stuffed'. Henry had eaten more modestly and the constable had been somewhat surprised when, after he'd finished what he wanted, he shoved the plate in Mickey's direction and Mickey helped himself to extra potatoes.

'Waste not, want not,' Mickey told him cheerfully when he saw him looking. He and Henry were so familiar with one another that sometimes they forgot other people might see their relationship as odd or wantonly informal.

'Did I see Sergeant Frith leaving?' the constable asked.

'You probably did. Do you know the man well?'

'Used to. Before he moved on and got promoted.'

Mickey raised an eyebrow. There was an edge of disapproval in the constable's tone. 'I take it you do not like him very much,' he said bluntly.

Constable Hargreaves coloured, his already florid nose becoming a little redder. 'I never said that, only that he'd moved on and got himself promoted.' He paused and thought about it for a moment and then said, 'You could say he's better at the political side than I would ever be.'

Mickey laughed, and let it lie. Henry had laid the ledgers on the table. Foolscap size and leather bound and filled with the constable's small and surprisingly neat hand. He was clearly assiduous in his note taking and the level of detail was impressive, including scraps of conversation overheard or reported or recorded, and he had followed up most of his small cases and detailed the outcome, even if the person concerned had moved elsewhere.

Henry commented on this and was told solemnly, 'This is my patch, my ground and my people. I grew up amongst them. I might not be the brightest and the best, but I care what happens round here, so of course I will make a note of it.'

'I count that as being bright enough and best enough,' Henry told him. 'Now the question is, where should we begin? Your books go back thirty or so years?'

The constable nodded. 'I joined up as soon as I was old enough. The old constable, he saw I had a better hand than he had, so he handed the note making over to me and I've been doing it ever since. We tend to be autonomous here; most of the local constables tend to mind their own patch and give help only when needed. In more remote places, we might be the only law for miles round. In winter the nearest law apart from us might be days away if we get cut off, so we have to be self-reliant, you see?'

'And so where do you suggest we begin?' Henry asked.

'And what's in the box?' Mickey added.

'Now, the box contains all of my clippings and all of my additional notes. Sometimes a bit of news might come to me that has nothing to do with official channels, so I write it down anyway but don't put it in the ledger because it's not official, if you get my thinking.'

'Indeed I do,' Mickey said. 'Right,' he added, rubbing his hands together. 'I think I'll get another round and then I'll take the box and my inspector here can work through the ledgers and you can give commentary on both.'

He picked up glasses and bustled off back to the bar, leaving Henry looking at the close, cramped and detailed hand, thinking that perhaps he had the worst part of the deal.

The Crown had filled up with local customers and a few who had travelled in from slightly further afield, seeking shelter for the night. Henry and Mickey had the best rooms but there were two kept for commercial travellers and the like who wanted cheap and cheerful and a good breakfast in the morning.

It was as if there was a cordon around their little corner. Only feet away people chatted and shouted and played bar billiards and laughed and drank, and then there was an empty space and then the three police officers with their box and books and notes.

Henry read the accounts of land disputes and family quarrels. Of Friday night fights and poachers brought before the magistrates. A man had shot his daughter when he'd discovered she was pregnant and unwed and her funeral had been attended by an estimated three hundred people, so many that the church could not hold them all. Henry wondered, somewhat cynically perhaps, how many would have turned up for the baptism, had her child been born, or how many would have attended the wedding, had she and her young man been able to tie the knot.

There were wrecked boats and deaths from exposure. A man had fallen from his bicycle into a ditch and drowned. The coroner had ruled accidental death but the constable's note said that the man had been depressed and his family reported him missing. 'It was a kindness on the part of the coroner,' he had added, noting also that the man was not local.

Despite his initial misgivings, Henry found himself oddly drawn to these small narratives and he began to look on the constable more warmly. This was not a man like Frith, set on promotion; he was far too rooted in his local community for that.

It was, though, the box that provided the first clue, in a bundle of clippings about a mysterious fire which had burned down a cottage and outbuildings only five miles from the village of Upchurch. There had been fears that the family of four had still been inside, but no bodies had been found and later there were reports of a car and a cart driving away at the time the fire was set.

'What's this?' Mickey asked.

'Ah, yes. I remember that. Strange business it was. First thought was that there was a fire with the people inside, and that they might have burned to death. Man, woman, two kiddies. Then there was the idea that they might have done a flit and for some reason set the cottage on fire, but their rent was paid up and paid in advance, and there had never been any problems with the tenancy, at least not until the man came back.'

'Came back?'

'End of the war; he'd been away. Only been back a short time, from what I recall. The odd thing is, the cottage was then on Cooper land. Where we borrowed the cart. They sold off that parcel only about a year later, though the farmer who bought it, a neighbour of theirs, had wanted it for a while as it gave him better access to his upper fields.'

Henry reached for a bundle of cuttings and flicked through them, finding the family names. 'The head of the household was Manfrid Beaney,' he said. 'The wife is recorded as Dalina and the children Kem and Malina. Unusual names.'

'Manfrid Beaney was a hellraiser,' the constable said. 'I was called out there three, four times after he got back from the war. He'd get drunk and beat his wife and kids. Not so unusual, but he was a little more extreme than the norm, if you get my meaning. If I remember right, when we got to the house we half expected to find him inside and the wife and kids gone. I don't know anyone would have blamed her and I was relieved when it wasn't so. I didn't want to punish a woman for what this man had done, maybe pushed her too far one day. But a crime would still be a crime, if she had done for him.'

'And they are unusual names.' Mickey returned to Henry's comment. 'Manfrid almost sounds German.'

The constable shook his head. 'Gypsy names,' he said. And he opened his eyes wide as though something had suddenly hit him. 'Our link to the camp,' he said. 'And if this Bailey chap, if he sent his men down to the encampment—'

'We have a possible, if tenuous, link,' Henry confirmed. 'This car and cart that were seen, were they ever followed up?'

'No. My notes will be in the book, but from memory I think there was only one sighting, and that by someone who was toddling home from the pub and so somewhat suspect as far as accuracy is concerned.'

Henry flicked through the second ledger and found the entry

for that night. It was as thorough and meticulous as all the rest, and the sighting of the wagon and the car had been added – and dated – three days after the events. 'The witness was a man called Tobias Wilson.'

'Long since passed, died of pneumonia a few winters ago. I know it, because he lived down the street from me in his final years. Moved in with his daughter.'

'Nothing was heard from the Beaneys. They contacted no family members round here, no friends?'

'Not as far as I know. Disappeared into the night and that was that.'

Henry had been leafing through the pages for any further account. 'The owner of the cottage was not best pleased and did go looking for them, and you have assumed here that he wanted to bring it all to court,' he said. 'But it seems they could not be found. And it seems that he was left uncompensated.'

'You say you went out to the cottage, on account of Manfrid's violence. That will be in your ledgers too?' Mickey asked.

'Of course it will. Now let me look.' For a minute or two he flicked back through the pages and marked four incidents. 'Each time he was given a warning, and each time he ignored it. If you look here I told the woman that she could bring him to court, that I was willing to arrest him. A man might give a woman a slap, and there are some women who give a man an odd slap, but that's not the same as taking your fists to a woman, beating and kicking.'

'So you thought she might have taken the law into her own hands. That's a fair assumption to have made, but you looked no further for her?'

For a moment, but only for that moment, the constable looked uncomfortable. 'I made the usual enquiries,' he said, 'but there was neither hair nor hide of them anywhere.' He paused to flick through his pages once again. 'According to this I put out word for them at the gypsy camp, but no word came back. The woman had family there, it seems.'

'And they would have closed ranks as soon as the enquiries were made,' Mickey commented.

'Quite likely they would. It's a way off my patch, I asked the locals to look at it and they told me nothing doing. So I accepted that.'

The threads were slowly starting to twist together, Henry thought. He had the strange feeling they might twist into a tight and round enough bundle to form a rope. A rope for someone's neck, perhaps.

SIXTEEN

After breakfast on the Wednesday morning, Henry and Mickey drove to Ash Tree Lane. By rights they should have informed Sergeant Frith that this was what they planned to do and it was a breach in protocol for them to go alone, but Mickey did not broach the subject and Henry did not mention it.

They parked up close to the gate and waited for somebody to come and speak to them, and then asked to see Sarah Cooper. The man at the gate glanced at their credentials and then beckoned them inside and they followed him through the camp. Henry looked around, keenly interested. There were many children running here and there and people set on their daily activities, building and tending fires, cooking, dealing with the horses. Most glanced in their direction as he and Mickey walked through and then turned away as though deliberately ignoring them. Only the children showed undisguised interest in the strangers and by the time they reached Sarah's vardo they had picked up a procession of tots and teens, who scattered when Sarah opened the door and glared at them. The man, his job apparently done, left them to Sarah's tender mercies.

'And who might you be? Obviously, the police.' She glanced beyond them and looked around, and then said, 'And where's Sergeant Frith got to?'

'You just have us this morning,' Mickey said pleasantly. 'Detective Sergeant Mickey Hitchens, and this is my boss Detective Chief Inspector Johnstone.'

'Well, there's fancy. And to what do we owe the pleasure?'

'You're sister to the late Mrs Beaney,' Henry said.

Sarah eyed him suspiciously. 'I told her after her old man died she should have changed her name back. It was her name, Cooper; she should have kept it.'

Mickey was curious. 'So Cooper is not your married name?'

'Cooper is *my* name. If my husband wished to take it, he could. What brothers I had died in the war, so there's no one to carry the name forward for our branch of the family and it's now mine to do with as I wish.'

'We are told you had a strange visit the night before last,' Mickey said. 'A group of men in three cars, carrying guns. Apparently they left swiftly, with their tails between their legs. What did they want with you, Sarah Cooper?'

'And who says they wanted anything with me? The only visitors we had two nights ago were a rabble of young 'uns, followed some of ours back after they'd been drinking together, caused a bit of a ruckus and went on their way.'

'That doesn't fit with what we've been told. With what a witness has told.'

'What witness? You're wasting your time, coming here. What can we tell you?'

'I don't know,' Henry said. 'What can you tell us? Or perhaps we should begin by telling you what we know?'

The woman looked at him, head slightly on one side, undecided about what to do with him, and then she shrugged. 'Get along with it, then. I don't have time to waste.'

Henry's attention had been attracted by something happening over on the far side of the camp and now he began to walk towards it, leaving a puzzled Mickey and a very annoyed Sarah in his wake. Two young men were sparring in an improvised ring made of hay bales and they had quite an audience. They were bare fisted, fast and disciplined. The aim seemed to be to test one another out, not to do damage or even score points at this stage, and to Henry's practised eye it was clear that these two were strangers to one another and had probably not yet battled for real.

Watching closely was a much older man, wearing a heavy coat and a flat cap. His face was lined with wrinkles upon wrinkles, but his body moved in sympathy with those of the young men, jabbing and dodging and ducking, his left hand fetching round into a vicious uppercut that contacted nothing but seemed to make the air shiver.

Sarah looked amused. 'Fancy your chances, do you, copper?'

Mickey just laughed.

Henry turned and looked at the woman thoughtfully and then he nodded. 'Why not?'

More laughter. This time the men watching the boxers joined in as they realized there was amusement to be had. Mickey was careful not to react.

Henry shed his coat, jacket, waistcoat and shirt, leaving just his short-sleeved singlet. He eased his feet out of his shoes and stepped forward into the ring. The two young men had stopped, unsure of what to do next. The old man called them aside and threw blankets round their shoulders so they didn't take cold while they were waiting. Henry was soon joined by another man, the one who had escorted them from the gate. Sarah plonked herself down on one of the hay bales, swung her legs over so that she was facing the ring, and Mickey, more cautiously, sat beside her. 'They don't like the women to watch the fighting,' she said. 'Not a woman's place – but neither is it a policeman's.'

'He lives by his own rules,' Mickey told her. But these were strange rules, even by Henry's standards.

The mood changed. Whereas the two boys had been trying each other out, testing boundaries and speed and skill, the two men who now moved in the ring seemed to have other concerns. It was a long time since Mickey had seen the scars on Henry's arms and shoulders. They were clearly from burns and stood out whiter than ever against pale skin. The other man had been browned by many summers out on the roads, his skin still tanned even in the depths of winter. They were well matched for height and reach, Mickey thought.

There was a strange silence as the two men began to move, dancing around one another. After all, it wasn't every day you saw one of yours get the chance to hit a policeman and not get banged up for it. Henry moved first, jabbing with his right and then following through immediately with a left uppercut. He made contact, but not hard. Bare knuckled you don't focus on the head, at least not in the early part of the fight. Bones are hard and can wreck knuckles, so it's body shots you go for, wearing your opponent down. But he had proved his point, got inside the other man's guard, and now the fight was on in earnest. A flurry of blows from either side followed, sharp and jabby; not hard, but intended to demonstrate what speed each man had, what skill. Only when this had been established did they follow through and the slap of knuckle on muscle seemed very loud in the tense silence.

Henry was more than holding his own. The other man was tough and wiry, but he was also impatient and a little put out to find himself matched when he hoped to be superior. Henry landed three forceful body blows, one after the other, following through with the full force of what little weight he had and driving his opponent back towards the perimeter. His opponent twisted, turned and aimed a kidney punch but Henry was quick enough to avoid it landing fully and moved forward, catching his opponent's foot as he did so, and the man almost went down.

Almost, but not quite. And he was angry now, and the anger fuelled his punches. Two landed hard on Henry's sternum and then a third, below, caught him in the diaphragm. Henry returned the blows in kind, though he was gasping for breath now. Mickey held his own breath as his boss suddenly lurched forward beneath the other man's guard and jabbed first in the ear and then in the jaw, sending him staggering.

Henry backed off then, leaning forward to catch his breath. His knuckles were bleeding and his opponent looked dazed. The old man who'd been watching the boys fight came forward and threw a towel on the ground between the two fighters.

'Enough,' he said. 'You've both had your fun – now bugger off. I've work to do.'

For a moment both men looked reluctant; then they realized that they'd been told, and that everybody expected them to take notice.

Sarah was laughing as Henry came back to retrieve his clothes. 'Well,' she said, 'that's something I've never seen before. And like as not, will never see again. Have fun, did you?'

Henry fastened his shirt and replaced his waistcoat and jacket before walking over to one of the nearby bales and sitting down so that he could put on his shoes.

'In December 1918,' he said, 'your sister Dalina Beaney and her children turned up here one very cold night and you took them in. The cottage had been burned down and everybody assumed that at least one body would be inside. Many people thought she'd killed her husband and set fire to the cottage to cover up the crime, or at least that's what the local constable told me. But as it happened, there was no one inside. What had happened to the husband I do not know, but your sister and her children walked here, and you took them in. That much I know, because of enquiries that were made subsequently. And so the local constabulary came and enquired after her, and finding her and the children safe took no more action – or perhaps they came asking but were sent away, still in a state of ignorance. She said, according to the reports, that her husband had left and she didn't know where he'd gone. The local farmer who owned the cottage that had been burned down said that previously she was a good tenant. He was left out of pocket by the whole experience, but no more action was taken against your sister or her children, presumably because it was your brother-in-law who was named on the rental agreement. Or was it that the Coopers who owned the cottage and the land were also kin?

'We know that your brother-in-law went away to the war in 1915. I don't know what regiment he was with because I haven't looked that far yet, and it wasn't in the reports that I've been shown. We know also that the marriage was an unhappy one, because the local constable had been called out to the cottage to deal with violent incidents on several occasions since his return. Hence the suspicion that your sister might have done away with him and burned the cottage down to hide her crime.

'I suspect she may well have done away with him. The man was a thoroughly bad lot. From all accounts, he was also a known associate of one Josiah Bailey. I'm sure you know the name.'

'And why should I know the name?'

'Because Bailey's men came here two nights ago. The only reason I can think of that they might have come here is that they were looking for your sister. Why they were looking for your sister is yet a mystery to me, but it's significant that two of Bailey's men fetched up dead at Otterham Creek last week, not more than a mile from where your sister was living ten years ago.'

'*Was* living. *Ten years* ago. It's nothing to do with her now, and besides, she's been dead this last five years.'

'And the children?'

'Grown up and gone on their way, as children do.'

Henry shrugged into his overcoat and cast a long, thoughtful glance around the encampment. 'I'm told some people live here full time, that they have mailing addresses and plots designated for them. I'm told that others pass through, and that most of the permanent inhabitants as well as the passers through work on agricultural land during the summer. Also, that this time of year showmen from the circus and fairgrounds tend to use this as a passing place. And that this is a stable community which causes little trouble and certainly wants none.'

'And all of that is true,' Sarah told him.

'That being the case, you should take warning. Josiah Bailey is not a man to be taken lightly and if he wants something from you, then he will take it.'

She seemed to come to a decision. 'His men didn't do so well the other night.'

'And no doubt those who failed will be suffering for it even now. But others will come. They won't rest until they have whatever they are looking for, whoever they are looking for – because Bailey won't allow them to. You understand me.'

She nodded. 'Then we'll be ready for them.'

'Perhaps. Perhaps not. Either way it will go badly for everyone, you may take my word on that. And you would do well to warn those two, your sister's children, because if he suspects they might know the truth of whatever it is he's looking for, their lives are worth nothing.'

His words had affected her, he could see, but she faced him down boldly and didn't flinch.

'Thank your man for the bruises,' Henry said. He headed back towards the gate, Mickey in tow.

She called out to him, just before they reached the perimeter.

'Kem and Malina,' she said. 'Cooper. They took back their

family name, but I think my sister kept her married one as a penance – though believe me, I have no idea for what.'

Henry paused, but did not turn.

'She's rooming at the residential club on Guilford Street and he's on the boats. On the *Lady Bay*.'

'Thank you,' Henry said. 'Now look to your people here. Warn them.'

Once they were a little distance away Mickey said, 'You know, you can be an idiot. Sometimes.'

Henry felt his bruised ribs gingerly. 'I'm aware of that fact,' he said.

They had the address of the reported witness, the boy who claimed to have seen armed men getting out of three cars and heading into the gypsy camp.

'I thought Sergeant Frith would be coming back,' Mrs Barclay said as she scrutinized their identity cards and at last decided to let them through the front door. She was, Henry thought, a solid woman. Tall and upright and, he imagined, usually quite immovable. He wondered what Mr Barclay might be like and whether he found ways to circumvent his wife or was constantly either pushing against her or being pushed back.

In his next moment he wondered if he was being unfair. No doubt Mickey would have plenty to say later on, and once he'd heard Mickey's opinion he might revise his own.

The woman led them into a parlour, unheated and clearly little used, obviously reserved for high days and holidays and visiting vicars. It seemed that visiting police officers came into the same category.

'You may as well sit down,' she said. 'My boy's at school. I don't know what you expected in the middle of the day. It's all very well for those children over there not to go to school, but mine is a respectable boy.'

Henry realized that it hadn't even occurred to him that the boy might not be there, but of course it was a school day. He sat down in one of the beautifully upholstered wing chairs. Both were of green leather and looked as though they had escaped from a gentlemen's club, button backed and with outswept arms. Mickey took the other and they faced her across a woven Turkish rug that was set before the hearth. The rug was the one bright thing in the room, reds and deep blues and little shots of green that he felt should have told him something about where it was made, but he could not quite call the information to mind. Cynthia would have known immediately.

Henry wondered if the fire was ever lit in here and decided from the general feeling of damp that it probably was not. He was glad of his coat.

Mrs Barclay seemed immune to it; in her red dress and dark cardigan she seemed quite at ease.

'We are interested to hear what your son has to say,' Henry said. 'And we are quite content to come back at a time convenient to yourself, and to your son. When does the school finish for the day?'

'I'm afraid it would not be convenient. Not at any time. I've already told Sergeant Frith, and so has Cedric, all the boy claims to have seen that night.'

'Claims to have seen?' Mickey enquired. 'You don't believe your son, then?'

She glared at him. 'My son is not a liar. But he does let his imagination run away from him and he does read too many American books. What the local library is doing allowing a child to borrow such trash I do not know. It just feeds their imagination and boys of that age have far too much as it is. Another few months and he will be out to work and so much the better. It'll give him far less time to think.'

The thought dawned on Henry: she is frightened. And she is lying. It seemed it must be his day for impulsive actions, because he got up and walked to the door and then went out into the narrow wood-panelled hallway. It was an Edwardian house, a larger terrace at the end, with a garden that wrapped around on three sides. As with most houses of this design, there was a front parlour and, he guessed, a middle room and then the kitchen. Henry opened the door to the middle room. 'Cedric,' he said. 'I think you should come out now.'

Behind him, Mrs Barclay was incandescent. She spluttered and shouted and told Henry that he had no right. Henry ignored her, and Cedric stepped through from the kitchen beyond, where he'd been hiding.

'Sit down, Cedric,' Henry told him. 'Not at school, then?'

The boy was looking at his mother for direction and Henry could feel her fury at his back, but he stepped inside the middle room and directed the boy to a chair and Mrs Barclay to another. 'You lied to me,' he said. 'That could be classed as obstruction, Mrs Barclay. It could be construed as a criminal offence.'

Cedric asked, 'You won't arrest my mother?'

Henry turned on him eyes that were as cold and grey as river pebbles and the boy quailed; so did his mother. 'I do not like being taken for a fool,' he said. 'Now, the truth of what you saw.'

The immovable wall that had been Mrs Barclay now crumbled and she took her son's hand. 'You better tell them, Ceddie dear,' she said. 'You better tell these . . . people . . . what you saw.'

Henry continued to hold them with his gaze, cold and hard. He could be harsh sometimes, Mickey thought, and he himself said more gently, 'Cedric, what time was it when you saw the cars?'

'I'm not sure, about one o'clock, I think. There were three cars in the park just up the road. They'd cut the engines and were coasting down, and that's what I thought was strange. They'd turned the lights out too, like they didn't want anybody to see them.'

'You have any idea what the cars might have been, or did you notice the registration on them?'

'No. It was too dark for that. But I saw the men get out and as they moved under the street light I saw that two of them were holding guns in their hands, and some of the others had things like sticks and metal bars.'

'And they didn't see you?'

Cedric shook his head violently. 'I saw them and I dodged back from the window. Mister, I was scared. I saw them split up – three go one way, three go the other and the others go towards the gate. But I could only see to the end of the road, you can just see the gate from here, from my room.'

'I'd like you to show me,' Mickey said.

Mrs Barclay looked ready to object. But she took another look at Henry and conceded defeat. She nodded at her son and Mickey and Cedric made their way upstairs. Henry stayed put.

'And when will Mr Barclay be home . . . or is he too hiding somewhere in this house?'

Her expression was laden now with utter loathing and contempt. He had crossed a line. 'My husband died. In 1917, my husband died. He left me with a two-year-old boy and, because he was an officer, a small pension. I have fought tooth and nail to raise my son, and to raise him properly so that he can take his place in the world and earn an honest living. I have skill at dressmaking and tailoring, and that has seen us through.'

She turned her face away from Henry and pointedly ignored him until Mickey and her son returned.

'I don't think there's much more that Cedric can tell us,' Mickey said, taking in the frosty silence.

Henry rose and thanked the woman formally and he and Mickey left.

'What the devil's got into you today?' Mickey demanded as they walked back to the car. 'First that tomfoolery at the gypsy camp, and now that. The woman was not a *suspect*.'

'Perhaps not. But she lied to us.'

'You'll find nothing as protective as a mother, you know that. Or you should do, knowing your Cynthia. She was frightened, Henry. When people are afraid they act in what they see as their own best interests, not in ours, you know that.'

Henry shrugged. 'What could be seen from the boy's room?'

'What he said. A little of the gate, and a little of the road as it turns uphill. So, they came up, mob handed, and they came armed. There would have been broken heads and, if there were gunshots, perhaps dead too, but as neither side is prepared to tell us anything useful . . .'

'Pieces begin to fall into place,' Henry said thoughtfully. 'And you are right, I behaved badly. To the woman, anyway.'

'And if word of this gets back, any of it, it will show neither of us in a good light.'

'If it does, then I will shoulder the blame,' Henry said with equanimity.

'Lord, but you can be an awkward bastard when the mood takes you,' Mickey said.

There were two messages waiting for Henry when they arrived back at the Crown. The first had been sent down from central office and was information that he'd asked for, but he was very surprised to recognize his niece's hand on the second letter. He'd left Cynthia the pub's address, just in case she needed to reach him, and she must have allowed Melissa to use it. Melissa and Henry had a regular correspondence. He took the letter upstairs and waited until he'd run a bath before opening it. He settled into the bath, hoping to ease his bruises and telling himself that he had in fact been a complete idiot and that Mickey was right and he deserved the reprimand. Opening the letter, he found that there was also an enclosure from Cynthia; just a quick loving greeting, but he was glad of it.

> *Dear Uncle Henry,* Melissa wrote,
>
> *I learned something interesting today from Nanny. I asked what it meant when people talked about kith and kin. I know kin means family and Nanny said that kin means people who are blood relations to you or who are accepted as family even though they might not be blood relations, but kith is people that you are meant to be couth to. Nanny told me that the word comes from couth and uncouth, and that it is probably Anglo-Saxon.*
>
> *Don't you think it's funny, Uncle Henry, that some words have come to be only used one way now and not the opposite? We talk about uncouth, but we very rarely say anybody is couth. At least I've never heard anybody say that somebody is couth, but Nanny says that is because the word has become kith. She said it had transmuted. I had to ask how to spell that. It's like gormless. Nanny likes the word gormless, but she tells me that gorm is also a word, that somebody can be gormful or gormless.*
>
> *Uncle Henry, I think you are thoroughly gormful.*
>
> *I am looking forward to our shopping trip. I am also*

looking forward to Cyril coming home at the end of this week.

Your faithful niece, Melissa

Henry laughed aloud and then realized that his ribs hurt when he laughed, so he stopped. 'If you'd seen me today, Melissa, you would have decided on gormless rather than gormful, I think,' he said.

When he arrived downstairs he found that Mickey had been doing his best, using the pub telephone, to contact Malina Cooper, and had finally got through. His suspicions aroused at a voice he did not recognize, the caretaker had not been at all sure that Mickey's credentials were correct when he had told him that he was a police officer. He'd also been very concerned that the young lady might be in trouble, or that something might have happened to her brother or her family, and when Malina finally came to the phone Mickey could imagine the man hovering in the background and listening to the conversation.

'I told her we paid a visit to her Aunt Sarah and that we were concerned for her welfare. She took some convincing, but she's finally agreed to meet us, though she didn't want to meet until Kem could be with her. As she is not due to have contact with him again before this Sunday I was at pains to insist she see us sooner, and she finally agreed that after work tomorrow she and a friend will convene to a Lyons' Corner House and she'll listen to what we have to say.'

'And is she cut from the same cloth as her aunt?'

'Oh, very much so, I would say. How are the ribs and the knuckles?'

'As you would expect,' Henry confessed. 'I forget sometimes that I am no longer a young man.'

'You're not an old man either, but you *are* old enough to have more sense.'

'So,' Mickey said, when they had settled in their usual corner. 'Time to collate what we have, I think. What we know so far, and what we don't.'

Henry nodded, taking his notebook from his pocket and setting it on the table beside an open map.

Mickey was flicking through his own notebook. 'Right,' he said. 'So on Wednesday last, the fifth of December, we were called out to examine two bodies, brought ashore at' – he pointed at the map – 'approximately this point, here. The initial story was that they had been found deeper in the channel and brought to shore by a man and boy who called themselves Frederick and Eddy Garth, Eddy being the boy, and claimed they were skipper and third hand aboard a sailing barge called the *Delilah*.'

'A story which is untrue in most of its detail,' Henry continued. 'And this' – he unfolded the communication that had been waiting for him on their return to the Crown – 'indicates that the *Delilah*, though she certainly exists, is not a sailing barge but a lighter. And they have no crew aboard of that name, and they have never had crew aboard of that name. So far we have no one who recognizes the photographs either.

'As the constable told us, lighters are flat-bottomed barges, generally used within docks to row goods and people to and fro. An unpowered lighter would not be out in the middle of the Medway and would be unlikely to be found even in Otterham Creek.'

'But that's not to say our man might not have been a lighterman at some point,' Mickey suggested. 'We know that people resort to half truths rather than full lies because it helps keep the story straight. So it's still worth pursuing.'

'Very true, and it will take time. There are a lot of docklands to search in the Thames and the Medway, and a lot of people to question, and it is an itinerant population.'

'So,' Mickey continued, 'we know the identities of both men, Billy Crane and Max Peterson, and we know that Billy Crane was one of Bailey's crew and we have it on information from Thomas Boswell that Crane was, as he put it, a "favoured child". Probably an actual illegitimate child of Bailey's and so he's likely to take this personally. I'm inclining towards the idea that Bailey was not responsible for these two deaths, but only for that of Grigor Vardanyan.'

'On balance, I agree with that analysis. But that third death, our little Armenian informant and card-sharp, that certainly bears all the hallmarks of Josiah Bailey and his gang.'

'So this brings us to the information from ten years ago, when the Beaney family were burned out of their home and taken elsewhere – if we are to believe in the witness statement about the wagon and the car. A story we cannot test or prove. On the other hand, why would anyone lie about such a thing?'

'And,' Henry added, 'we now know that Dalina Beaney and her children made their way to the gypsy encampment at Ash Tree Lane and that their family took them in and cared for them. That Dalina died there. We must get a death certificate to establish that point, but I see no immediate reason to doubt it.'

'It's quite likely the children will have a copy anyway,' Mickey asserted. 'And we'll gain more knowledge of that end of things when we meet the daughter tomorrow. But now we begin to get strange. Bailey, and we must assume that it was Bailey at this point, sends twelve armed men out in search of Dalina Beaney. Only twelve, which in the context of the size of the encampment seems a little inadequate, and perhaps speaks to lack of knowledge or intelligence, or both. And speculating purely on coincidence, I would guess that the name was given to him by Grigor Vardanyan. Now that name could mean something or nothing. He was beaten so badly he'd have said anything, but we also have the coincidence of location, of the Beaney family being driven out and of the finding of Bailey's two men close by that spot.'

'And given that the cottage was probably owned by kin of Dalina's, that makes me think she saw it as a safe haven, away from Bailey and the life she had lived with her husband in London. Perhaps she hoped that he would not return from the war.'

'The devil looks after his own,' Mickey said morosely.

'We both came back.'

'I rest my case.'

'We can't see all the permutations yet, all the connections,' Henry added, 'though the shadows of connections are beginning to emerge. But I'm troubled by the violence meted out on the little card-sharp. Either he held out for a long period of time or he gave the wrong information; he told Bailey what he did not want to hear.'

'Perhaps he didn't know exactly what it was that Bailey wanted – and perhaps Bailey didn't either.'

'So then, we have the boy Cedric seeing these men arrive and telling his mother. We have the mother reporting this to Sergeant Frith, who then blabs the information at the gypsy camp. Now we've no reason to believe that there is a connection between the encampment and Bailey – in fact, quite the opposite – but that doesn't excuse Frith talking about a witness when it's obvious that only those overlooking the street on the night of the attack could possibly have witnessed anything. That's a handful of people; it would be easy for anyone to discover who this witness was and what they had seen. At the very least, it is careless and unprofessional.'

Mickey raised his glass and drank, peering at his boss over the rim.

'I will not rise to that bait, Mickey. So, where do we go from here?'

'We speak to the girl. We keep looking for the man and boy. Do we know where Grigor was living?'

'That too was in the information sent today. He had a room above a clockmaker's shop. A man named Abraham Levy. He was interviewed today, but I would like to go and speak to him again.' Henry consulted the notes he had been sent. 'It seems he had not seen his tenant for three or four days, but that that was not unusual. He paid his rent and was a quiet tenant.'

'So tomorrow when we return to London, we will pay this Abraham Levy a visit.'

'And we need to find the young man, Kem Beaney, or Cooper as he is now.'

'His sister says that he is likely to be at sea until Friday or Saturday night. They plan to visit the mother's grave on Sunday,' Mickey told him. 'In the meantime we will see what his sister can tell us. Speaking of sisters, what did you make of Sarah Cooper?'

'Intelligent, loyal and tenacious,' Henry said. 'I am not surprised her sister went to her in times of trouble. I find it less likely that the sister did not confide in her, at least in some measure.'

'Do you mean to go and see her again?'

'Perhaps. We will find out what the children have to say first. It's possible the mother told them something before she died. The other thing that puzzles me is the method of killing. Billy Crane and Max Peterson were both killed by single stab wounds, but the method and the weapon were different in each case. One seems to be a knife, straightforward enough, and an accurate upward thrust which anyone with a little practice would be able to manage. The second is more puzzling. What weapon was used, and why? And I still draw parallels with the death of Martha Howells in January this year. That is still unsolved, and her body was probably only discovered by chance. It's quite likely it would have been swept away into the river after the floods, and no one would have been the wiser.'

'True,' Mickey agreed.

It had been Henry himself who had picked up the body and carried it to a point above where the floodwaters looked set to rise. He'd taken her into an old theatre building, and the water had come in much faster than anyone had anticipated, the Thames breaking banks, damaging walls and houses and drowning those in basements. Henry had been trapped with the body for fifteen hours before the waters receded enough for a boatman to reach them.

'And did she have a link to Bailey? Now there's a question no one had reason to ask at the time.'

Henry looked thoughtful and then shrugged. 'She was a prostitute, well known, and her associates were all interviewed. But – and this is one thing that surprised us all, if I remember – until recently, she'd worked out of a house in Princelet Street, along with three other girls. She was from the south of England, but of the other three one was Italian, one French and the other, I believe, was Dutch. It struck me as strange, but maybe not so strange. You know how many foreign nationals there are in the sex trade in London.'

Mickey nodded. 'And how many men there are that see these foreign girls as exotic. Safer to work from premises, I'd have thought, so why did she stop? Was that ever established?'

'As I remember, the girls just said she'd left about a week before she died. The woman who ran the house told us that girls come and go all the time, and she saw nothing strange in that. Or so she said.'

'This has always niggled you,' Mickey commented.

'You know I hate to leave things untied. All of this might be coincidence, of course.'

'It might be,' Mickey agreed. 'But you don't think so, and neither do I.'

SEVENTEEN

It could, Henry wrote in his journal, *be seen almost as a commonplace to find a prostitute dead, or for one to be assaulted. Such has been an occupational hazard probably for as long as prostitution has existed, but it is certainly so in the big cities, and London is no exception.*

On the night we found Martha Howells dead, she was one of two prostitutes discovered murdered. Because they were not victims of the flood they are not listed among the fourteen dead, casualties of poverty and natural disaster. But they were victims nonetheless. The other, whose name I do not recall because I was not directly involved, had been bludgeoned and her earnings stolen. But Martha Howells had been stabbed once, with a weapon of unusual shape which has not yet been identified.

I happened to be with a group of constables close to the foreshore – or what had been the foreshore before the water came in. I have to say it was a terrifying event. Poor families crammed into basements were inundated within moments and the lucky ones were pulled out by neighbours or by police officers or by passers-by. Many were trapped on higher floors and were left for hours without help, or water or heat. They were the lucky ones, in some ways. I remember we spotted this woman – or rather, we spotted her body – and the first assumption was that she was another drowning victim. Her clothes were sodden and her hair had fallen forward on to her face. She was lying face down on the ground and it was only when we turned her, to check for signs of life, that we saw the blood on her chest and realized that the cause of death was not drowning.

The water was coming in rapidly and the constables

with me were of more use helping with the evacuation, so we picked her up and carried her to higher ground. I can remember the roar as something gave way, I still can't be sure what, but the water was suddenly all around, and had risen from ankle deep up to my knees. Had we arrived any later her body would have been washed away and none been any the wiser.

Henry paused, remembering. That had been an appalling night. Dark and freezing, and most of those on patrol had spent it sodden and miserable, doing what they could for those who had lost everything.

But what had Martha Howells to do with Max Peterson and Billy Crane? It was not so neat a wound as that which I saw on this second body, that of Max Peterson. It was as though the woman had been in motion, turning perhaps when the blow had been struck. The man, bound and possibly even held still, had not moved and therefore the weapon had gone in straight and clean and so it looked, at first, like a bullet wound. The internal shape of both is the same, I am sure of it.

Was there a link, Henry wondered, or was he just looking for patterns where none existed?

The following morning they returned to London and delivered their initial reports and just after midday they went to visit Abraham Levy, the clockmaker over whose shop Grigor had lodged.

Abraham Levy was a tall man, lean and stern in appearance, but his voice and tone told another story. When they entered he was discussing a clock with a customer. 'You can leave it with me,' he said, 'but I'm warning you, it will be expensive. This clock has not been made, not been produced for fifty or sixty years. If I must make parts for it, then I must make parts for it. If the clock is precious enough to you, then I will make parts for it. I can give you an estimate and then you can say, Abraham, this is too much, and I won't take offence.'

He glanced up to look at the two men who had entered and then returned his attention to his customer. 'Maybe you should keep this clock just for the show of it? Maybe you should buy a new clock for telling the time. A clock that will tell you the right and proper time, and not what it thinks the time ought to be. Clocks are like people, when they get older they get forgetful.'

Abraham and the customer obviously knew each other well and the woman laughed. 'I will think about it, Abraham,' she said. 'And perhaps you are right, perhaps I should give my old forgetful clock a nice retirement and just buy myself a nice new clock. Perhaps one of those electric ones. Perhaps one without a pendulum.'

It was obvious to Mickey that this conversation picked up on old themes and that the woman was gently goading the clockmaker because Abraham threw up his hands in horror. 'A clock without a pendulum is a clock without a heart. My dear, you cannot be serious. I will find you a nice new clock, with a pendulum, with a good tick.'

'I will have to think about it,' she said. She picked up the box that must contain the errant clock and Henry held the door for her as she left.

'And you must be more policemen,' Abraham said. 'Two I had here yesterday, two more today, it seems. If you want to see the boy's room come through the back and go up the stairs. It is the second on the right.' He flipped up a panel in the counter and let them through and Mickey introduced them both.

'If you have a few moments, we would like to ask some questions,' Mickey said.

'Then when you come down I will have made tea,' Abraham told them. 'And I'll put the sign on the door to say that I'm closed for a little while and you can ask your questions – and I hope they are more intelligent questions than those idiot constables asked me yesterday.'

The stairs were narrow and uncarpeted, but the room itself was tidy and, though sparse, had everything that might be needed. A bed, a two-ring stove, a sink plumbed into the corner. To one side of the sink was a rack for draining pots and the shelf above held shaving gear, so the sink obviously served two purposes, the washing of both the person and his crockery.

'I've seen far worse living places,' Mickey commented. 'At least it's clean and there doesn't seem to be any damp.' He dumped his bag down on a chair and extracted the camera. 'Not much point looking for fingerprints,' he said, 'not if the constables were up here yesterday. We'd have to find them and fingerprint them for elimination and that would take Lord knows how long. And they'd object, you just know they would. I had one idiot say it made him feel like a criminal, last time I had to do that.'

He stopped grumbling and looked around. 'Besides,' he said, 'I suppose this poor little room doesn't fully count as a scene of crime. It won't take long to cover this, at any rate,' he said, surveying the tiny space. 'I wonder if there's another lodger in the second room.'

'Not likely to be there at this hour, if there is,' Henry said, 'but I'll take a look inside and we can talk to the clockmaker about it when we go down.'

He was back inside a few moments, reporting that the room appeared to be empty and unlived in. It was set out in a similar way to Grigor's. Mickey had begun to take photographs and Henry tracked him around the room, searching after Mickey had catalogued. It did not take them very long and the haul of items that went into manila envelopes and then into the murder bag was small. A few letters, some newspaper clippings, receipts from a tailor – for a shirt, to have its collar turned – and a pawnbroker, for a pocket watch. No money and no valuables. A few spare clothes, but it seemed that most of what Grigor owned he was wearing or carrying when he met his death.

They went back downstairs and Abraham let them through to a small back room. He took the kettle from the top of a barrel stove and filled the tea pot and then went back into the shop to turn the sign to closed ('Back in ten minutes'). He obviously expected them to take only a little of his day.

'So,' he said. 'You'll be wanting to ask me how long he lived here and I will tell you, about a month. You will be wanting to ask me how well I knew him and I will tell you, not well at all. He was quiet, he paid his rent mostly on time, he never made any trouble. Once he left for a few days and he told me he was going to be away. He said, Abraham, I will be away from Thursday through to Monday. This time he did not tell me he was going, and so I worried for him. Now it seems I was right to worry.'

'You say you did not know him very well and yet you worried for him. You liked him, then?' Mickey asked.

'I liked him as well as anyone can like a man they do not know very well, but who lives under their roof. Though technically my roof is next door, and usually I have two lodgers here. It's cheaper than keeping a guard dog and certainly cheaper than installing any kind of alarm system. Not that I have much faith in alarm systems. A good lock, now that is a good thing, and a good dog is another good thing. Two lodgers, even better.'

'And did you have two lodgers at this present time?'

Abraham shook his head. 'I had two. A young man called Anthony who left because his family needed him. That would be ten days or so ago and I can give you his address, should you need it. And poor, poor Grigor. Now I have no lodgers, and that young man has no life.'

Henry sat at his desk, Mickey opposite, and together they examined the items they had taken from Grigor's room. On the way back they had called at the tailor's and also the pawnbroker, where they retrieved a cheap brass pocket watch. The tailor's had proved to be a small business run out of the front room of one of the terraced houses, just a few doors down from Abraham's shop. A woman and her daughter did repairs, made over and mended, and sometimes made from scratch. They had removed the collar from the shirt, turned it so the wear was hidden on the inside and reattached the collar, sewing a strip of binding over the seam so that it was left smooth.

Henry, perhaps reminded of Mickey's act of kindness to the man and boy who claimed to have found the bodies, had felt obliged to pay for the work that had been done.

He was reminded also of the woman, Cedric's mother, whom

they had met the day before – though it was in his mind that she would not have made any kind of association between her own situation and the work done by this East End woman and her daughter. Mrs Barclay would have viewed herself as a cut above, Henry thought.

'According to the pawnbroker, the watch was in and out of hock at least once a month,' Mickey commented. 'And it's a perfectly ordinary watch, no inscription, no dents and scratches, as you'd expect if it's just been carried in a pocket. And the shirt is a perfectly ordinary shirt, probably bought second-hand, with a stitched-on collar like that.'

Henry nodded. It was still a commonplace for poorer people and working men to wear shirts with a small stand-up to which a starched linen or celluloid collar could be fixed for Sunday best. But the trade in second-hand clothing was a lively one and the shirt looked much mended and had obviously had a long life.

He looked up at Mickey, something striking him in what his sergeant had said. 'But Grigor had only been out of gaol for a little over a month. The pawnbroker told you it had been in and out of hock on a regular basis; that might well be true, but it can't have been Grigor who pawned it.'

'So, he did it for someone else? But he kept the pawn ticket. Or maybe he'd acquired the watch from someone, a payment of a debt, or he stole it – no, that's unlikely. The pawnbroker clearly knew the watch so he'd surely not have risked hocking it in a place where the real owner might have been able to see it.'

'Or the pawnbroker was wrong,' Henry suggested. He turned the watch in his hands. It was a very ordinary watch with a plain brass case, not scratched or dented, as it might be had someone simply kept it in their pocket. Mickey kept his in his waistcoat and it too was smooth and relatively unscathed, bar the one small dent that Mickey tolerated because of the memory attached to it.

'One plain brass watch looks pretty much like another. If he looked down his register and saw a regular entry for a brass watch, he might have made an erroneous assumption, I suppose.'